And who's going to save you, Finn…?

Finn didn't need the subconscious poke in the ribs. Women like Lucy weren't part of his blueprint for life—he dated women who, like him, were interested in a good time with no messy emotional complications. The moment they wanted to bond with his son or started stopping outside jewelery stores with prominent ring displays, they were history. Lucy Foster had to be the world's epicenter of emotional complications! Getting involved with her would be about as sensible as pitching your tent on top of Mount Etna!

KIM LAWRENCE lives on a farm in rural Anglesey, Wales. She runs two miles daily and finds this an excellent opportunity to unwind and seek inspiration for her writing! It also helps her keep up with her husband, two active sons and the various stray animals that have adopted them. Always a fanatical consumer of fiction, she is now equally enthusiastic about writing. She loves a happy ending!

AT THE PLAYBOY'S PLEASURE

KIM LAWRENCE

THE MILLIONAIRE AFFAIR

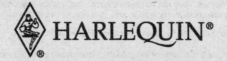

HARLEQUIN®

TORONTO • NEW YORK • LONDON
AMSTERDAM • PARIS • SYDNEY • HAMBURG
STOCKHOLM • ATHENS • TOKYO • MILAN • MADRID
PRAGUE • WARSAW • BUDAPEST • AUCKLAND

ISBN 0-373-82030-5

AT THE PLAYBOY'S PLEASURE

First North American Publication 2004.

Copyright © 2003 by Kim Lawrence.

This edition published by arrangement with Harlequin Books S.A.

® and TM are trademarks of the publisher. Trademarks indicated with ® are registered in the United States Patent and Trademark Office, the Canadian Trade Marks Office and in other countries.

www.eHarlequin.com

Printed in U.S.A.

CHAPTER ONE

FOR the first twenty minutes of the phone call Lucy's total contribution consisted of a series of admiring grunts and the occasionally awed '*Really…!*'

Her sister Annie was in love, which Lucy knew meant you had to make the sort of allowances you would for anyone suffering from temporary insanity. No problem, Lucy could do that, but there were limits to her endurance and even had she been a card-carrying member of the hopeless-romantic society this conversation might have put her off her lunch.

Lucy Foster *wasn't* a hopeless romantic, and she had resorted to biting her tongue to stop herself blurting out something caustic that would most likely alienate her big sister forever.

She'd never met Connor Fitzgerald, but she already hated the sound of his name.

Like Annie, Lucy had once imagined there was some *special* man out there for her, she had even thought that she had found him! A lot more than two years separated the person who was having to bite back cynical retorts from the pathetically trusting creature she had been back then.

Nowadays Lucy worked on the assumption that men were for the most part shallow creatures not to be trusted with a grocery list let alone a girl's heart. This philosophy served her pretty well…two years and no emotional entanglements and all the angst that inevitably accompanied them.

Though it had a lot of bad press, celibacy had a lot to recommend it.

It would clearly have been useless at the moment to attempt to sell this successful formula to her sister; human nature being what it was, some things you just had to learn the hard way, Lucy admitted to herself regretfully. No, she'd just have to be there to pick up the pieces when the man of the moment, this *Connor*, broke poor Annie's heart. Even if the man sounded like a total pain.

As far as Lucy was concerned it was not so much of a case of *if* but *when*.

It wasn't as if she had a closed mind on the subject— she was prepared to concede there might be *some* rare exceptions to her grocery-list rule—but the chances of Annie striking lucky seemed pretty remote to her.

It was some relief when Annie, having presumably used up her daily quota of clichés, finally stopped waxing lyrical about the length of Connor's eyelashes, his incredible sense of humour and his general all-round superiority to every other man that had ever been born, and got on to the actual reason for her call.

'I just called to say knock them dead, Luce.'

'I'll do my best,' Lucy promised.

'So, are you nervous?'

'I wouldn't say that.' She also wouldn't say she was exactly wildly confident either, in fact there had been several occasions during the past few days when she regretted letting her sister wangle her an interview for a job she was patently unqualified for. 'Well, actually, yes, I think I am slightly nervous…'

Running her tongue across her dry lips, she encountered the unexpected subtle taste of the expensive lipstick that had tinged her lips a fashionable shade of red—or so she'd been told by Marcus.

Lucy, in her total ignorance of this great man's fame, had created a minor furore in the salon frequented by numerous celebrities when she had asked him his surname. Well, his single name might be synonymous with excellence in the world of hairstyling and fashion but Lucy still felt doubtful about accepting style tips from a man the wrong side of forty who wore skin-tight black leather from head to toe!

'Well, adrenaline is good.'

Lucy wondered if she was the only one to find Annie's inexhaustible supply of optimism irritating. 'Even if it reduces me to a gibbering wreck?'

Lucy heard her sister give a sigh of exasperation. 'You remember that positive attitude we discussed?'

'I'm positive...*honestly*, I'm oozing confidence. I'll dazzle the interview panel with my wit, good looks and the sheer force of my stunning personality...' Which will make them overlook the fact a degree in modern history and working my way around Europe on a shoestring hardly qualifies me for a position as a PA in advertising.

'Now, that is *just* the sort of remark you want to avoid.'

'I was *joking*?'

'It's safer to assume that the people interviewing you don't have a sense of humour, dry or otherwise,' her sister advised. 'I'm beginning to think you're not taking this seriously. You do *want* a proper job?' Annie added, a note of critical doubt entering her voice.

'*Proper?*' Lucy yelped indignantly. 'What do you think I've been doing up until now?'

'Let me see, where shall I start? How about putting your life on hold for three years to act as an unpaid researcher for your boyfriend who then dumps you and takes the credit for all your work?' Lucy winced. That hadn't been her finest hour but she was older and wiser now.

'Or,' Annie continued warming to her theme, 'do you mean picking grapes in Burgundy? Or maybe looking after rich people's spoilt brats at Lucerne, and then there was the waitressing; now, that was a *great* career move…'

Lucy pulled a face down the receiver. 'They were *lovely* kids, and I got to see Europe.'

'I know, you saw the bits the tourists never see; call me superficial, love, but I like my authentic experience to involve *authentic* five-star hotels. And before you get all sniffy and superior think on…is it *so* bad of me wanting to see my little sister doing a decent job with some sort of prospects? It's such a waste—you were always the clever one…'

Too clever, Rupert had said when he had broken the news he had found a less clever and much prettier replacement. Lucy blinked away the painful memory.

'But you were the one with focus and drive.' It worried her slightly that the only thing her sister seemed driven to do at the moment was worship Connor Fitzgerald. 'Listen, I do appreciate what you're trying to do.'

'Good; so tell me, what are you wearing—the cream?'

'I don't have your cleavage to carry it off.'

'No, I don't suppose you do,' conceded the owner of a very superior cleavage.

'I'm wearing your black suit.' With typical generosity her sister had given Lucy the pick of her extensive wardrobe and the use of her flat for the duration of her stay in the capital.

'Well, I suppose anything's an improvement on your own clothes,' conceded Annie, who frequently despaired of getting her sister out of jeans. 'You did keep that appointment with Marcus?'

'I hardly recognise myself,' Lucy replied, lifting her eyes to the unfamiliar reflection in the mirror. 'If this is the *nat-*

ural look I dread to think what an unnatural one would look like!'

To achieve *natural* all minor trace of her freckles had been ruthlessly hidden behind several layers of pale matt foundation. In addition her choppily cut shoulder-length blonde hair been slicked back into a smooth chignon and her almond-shaped eyes dramatically outlined with dark liner that gave her an air of mystery.

'Looking as though you're not wearing any make-up takes time.'

'You're telling me, if I wanted to do this every day I'd have to get up at four a.m.'

'I thought you were a morning person.'

'But I'm not an exfoliating, moisturising and eyebrow-plucking person.'

Annie laughed at the piteous complaint. 'You just need practice. I told Marcus to give you the full works—hair, make-up, nails…not that you have any…'

'I do now,' Lucy replied with a dubious glance at the red talons where her short, unpolished nails had been earlier. 'And he gave me a doggy bag to take home with a bewildering selection of goodies.'

'A present from me for your new job.'

'I don't have the job yet…' Lucy felt impelled to remind her sister. She couldn't rid herself of the feeling she was going to be an awful disappointment.

'Oh, take it from me, you'll walk it. Now, are you feeding the cats? And you're not over-watering my plants? Oh, and if Derek from upstairs offers you a coffee don't say yes…he likes to pretend he's single when his wife goes to visit her mother.'

'The cats are fine, your plants are fine and I can promise I'll resist any of Derek's offers of coffee—especially if he is the one with the sloping shoulders, over-gelled hair and loud voice…or, for that matter even if he's not. Listen, Annie, there's someone at the door—I've got to go…'

'All right, but I'll ring later and you can tell me how you got on.'

'I will.'

It wasn't until Lucy had replaced the receiver that she remembered she had forgotten to ask for a contact number in case anything came up. Annie had mentioned the romantic ambience of the hotel but not the name—so all Lucy knew was that she was staying somewhere in the Lake District that had four-poster beds.

The door finally opened and Finn Fitzgerald saw that his worst fears had been more than realized. She was everything he'd been hoping not to find.

It seemed that when it came to a certain sort of blonde his kid brother was incapable of learning from his mistakes, even ones as emotionally and financially painful as two failed marriages—quite some record when you considered Con was still six months short of his thirtieth birthday!

Not only had his dismal experiences not put the romantically inclined Connor off the institute of marriage, but he was also *still* falling for the wrong sort of woman.

Not long out of college, Con had married Mia, a silvery ash-blonde eight years his senior with legs that went on forever. After twelve months Mia had left him for the job as head designer for a prestigious French fashion house without a backward glance.

Four years later Jasmine had come along. Another ash-blonde, Jasmine had been almost as fanatical about keeping her cellulite at bay as she had been at getting to the top and staying there even if it involved sleeping with the odd influential person on the way there. Which had proved problematic when her loving husband had come home to find her in bed with one, her boss of the moment.

Enough to put any sane man off marriage—but not his insanely optimistic brother!

This one certainly had everything his brother went for—long, shapely legs, a great body, cut-glass features and that inevitable untouchable aura. Finn didn't doubt for a moment she was as ruthless and self-centred as the previous two Mrs Fitzgeralds.

He sometimes wondered if Con's desire to thaw the ice and reveal the warm, vibrant woman beneath—*it hadn't sunk in yet that you couldn't discover something that wasn't there to begin with!*—went beyond the challenge and the legs?

A firm believer that a man made his own destiny and that you took responsibility for your own actions, Finn was normally highly resistant to the popular modern tendency to blame your character defects on a traumatic childhood incident. But when he considered his brother's history he couldn't help but wonder if there wasn't something in it.

Their parents had split up when he'd been ten and Con two years younger. The responsible adults had come up with the insane idea of dividing up the children along with the property, furniture and record collection.

He'd ended up with their mother, a tall blonde... *coincidence*? You didn't have to be Freud to see there was a theme here...a young kid felt rejected by his mother and in adult life tried to gain the love of women who bore more than a passing resemblance to her...self-centred...selfish... shallow...

He loved his mother dearly but he wasn't blind to the deficiencies in her character.

'Can I help you?' Lucy gave a smile, not her usual wide, warm smile, the one that lit up her face and wrinkled her eyes at the corners and would, according to Annie, lead to premature crow's feet, but a stiff little twitch of the lips.

It made her look worried and she was—worried that if she didn't leave soon she'd be late for her interview. Worried that when she got there she'd make a total fool of herself and worried that the innumerable layers that constituted her natural-looking make-up would develop irreparable cracks if she allowed herself the full range of facial expressions. The fear she would fall off the three-inch heels she hadn't quite got the hang of yet at a crucial moment was more a certainty than a worry. The highest heel Lucy wore as a rule was on her trainers.

The man who had been leaning with his hand pressed to the doorbell straightened upright. Lucy was forced to tilt her head back to make eye contact—she blinked as she encountered a pair of the bluest eyes she had ever seen.

The bewildering hostility she was seeing in those cerulean depths twitched her freshly tweaked eyebrows into a straight line—this was not the reaction her expensive makeover was supposed to have on the opposite sex.

Not that Lucy could imagine ever thinking it desirable to excite the admiration of a man like the one before her, who was everything she instinctively distrusted and disliked in a man.

He was the captain of the soccer team she had helped with his maths homework, but who couldn't remember her name in front of his mates. He was the man whose entrance into a room brought conversations to a halt. He was the man other men wanted to be and women just wanted.

For a moment Lucy was the tall, skinny, unhappy teenager with spots, who no boy would look at unless he wanted his homework done. Of course, she had had the last laugh. By the time they had reached their final year in school her skin had cleared up, she had filled out in all the right places and her A-level grades got her a full scholarship to university, but sweetest of all she had refused a date with the football captain.

Just looking at the man who brought all this back made her prickle with antagonism.

A lean and long, muscular six-four or -five with broad shoulders that nicely filled out the casual pale blue shirt he wore and long, *long* legs that equally nicely filled out the washed-out denims that were fastened with a leather belt around his narrow hips. In keeping with the blue theme his narrowed eyes with their fringe of ludicrously long jet lashes were the colour of a hot summer sky.

Add a broad, intelligent forehead, wide mouth, high cheekbones, a strong, straight nose and clear, lightly tanned skin stretched across a clean-shaven, aggressively strong jaw and you had an image that could have sold anything—always supposing the advertising folk were right when they said that sex could sell anything!

The only thing in her view that could redeem a man as good-looking as this specimen was him being charmingly oblivious to the fact he was as sexy as sin—a sweet, self-deprecating smile would help too. Something she judged to be about as likely as snow in July as she allowed her glance to dwell disapprovingly on the arrogant angle of the stranger's dark head and the cynical twist of his sculpted, overtly sensual lips.

Self-deprecating? *Hardly!*

Unaware of his appeal to the opposite sex? *Good joke!*

His body language was only slightly less indicative of smug self-satisfaction than neon letters across his intelligent-looking forehead. In sexual terms this guy was top of the food chain and, my God, did he know it! The day he didn't attract the expected number of second glances when he walked into a room he'd head for the nearest cosmetic surgeon.

The object of her growing contempt spoke, and his voice was in keeping with the rest of the package, a deep, gravelly drawl in which she could detect an attractive mingling of American and Irish.

'Miss Foster?'

'Yes, but…' Before she could launch into her explanation that she was *a* Miss Foster, but not the one he wanted, to her astonishment the tall stranger barged past her straight through the tiny hallway and into Annie's living room.

'Hey there!' Her cry brought no response. *'What do you think you're doing?'* she demanded, afforded a fleeting view of his broad shoulders. She just stopped herself inhaling to identify the subtle and attractive fragrance—warm male with a dash of something fresh and citrusy—that hung about his impressive person.

'Is he here?' The abrupt question was thrown over his shoulder as her uninvited guest, arms folded across his chest, assessed his surroundings in an offensively critical manner.

It wasn't until an astounded Lucy had indignantly followed him inside and heard the door slam behind her that it occurred to her that following him might not be the most sensible line of action. She almost turned and made a dash for safety, but when push came to shove she couldn't bring herself to abandon her sister's flat and belongings.

'Is who here?' It was probably wise to humour dangerous lunatics.

Lucy tried to consider the matter calmly; he was rude, he oozed arrogance, but, she told her jangling nerves, it didn't automatically follow that he was also dangerous— although if such things were judged in looks alone…

Her racing heart kicked up a further uncomfortable beat

as her eyes followed the panther-like progress of the intruder around the room. Lucy realised she had actually never encountered anyone who so perfectly embodied all the elements of danger as this man did—she never had understood why danger was such a turn-on for so many women; being in touching distance of it, she understood it even less!

She traced her tongue across the unsteady outline of her dry lips and tried not to let her over-active imagination get out of hand.

There was no need to assume the worst; there could be any number of perfectly good reasons for his unorthodox behaviour...*such as?*

Well, for instance, he could be Annie's past?

Lucy imperceptibly shook her head, experiencing a strong gut rejection of the idea. Not even Annie, with her weakness for a pretty face, was *that* stupid; this man had trouble written all over him.

It took her about two seconds to realise, much to her relief, that the lover theory didn't hold water. For starters if they'd been lovers he'd have hardly mistaken her for her curvaceous redheaded sister, and there was an even more fundamental flaw: her sister had never had a lover.

Though Lucy suspected that Annie had gone away to the Lakes that weekend with the intention of altering that particular situation!

Possibly there were some men around who dated a beautiful woman and didn't expect to sleep with her, but you didn't have to be a psychic to see this wasn't a man who was into platonic relationships. You only had to look at his mouth—Lucy did and immediately wished she hadn't—to see that he was an intensely sensual animal.

Feeling inexplicably relieved that her sister had never succumbed to this man's dark, dramatic charms, she watched, her thoughts racing and butterflies still running riot in her stomach, as he ignored her and continued to scan the small room as if expecting to discover someone concealed in a dark corner.

He picked up a signed photo of a good-looking pop star that Annie had successfully bid for at a charity auction. He read the fulsome personal message the boy had scrawled across it before replacing it.

He turned abruptly. 'Are you alone?'

Lucy, who had been studying his hands as he held the object, gave a startled gasp, she could hardly hear for the sound of warning bells going off in her head. With the best will in the world it was hard *not* to read all manner of sinister implications into that terse question.

She could recall reading somewhere that the worst thing you could do in front of dangerous animals was show fear. The same criteria might not apply with this stranger, whose fluid movements and soft-footed tread put her irresistibly in mind of some sleek jungle cat, but she wasn't taking any chances. Willing her face not to reflect her apprehension, she lifted her chin.

'My husband will be back any minute.' Would the law consider bashing someone over the head *reasonable force*?

Normally given to blushing madly when she lied, Lucy was surprised to hear herself sound quietly confident— maybe it was being dressed this way that made the difference. Like an actor who found it easier to get into character when in costume.

She had even begun considering elaborating on her partner's jealous temperament and prowess at martial arts when it became apparent that what she had said had already made a bigger impact than she had anticipated.

An expression of horror quite out of proportion with her

claim had spread across the demonically perfect features of the man opposite.

'Husband!' The muscles in his strong brown throat visibly spasmed.

His remarkable face could have been carved of stone, so still he became as his startling electric-blue eyes meshed with hers. Lucy found the mesmeric contact acutely uncomfortable but found herself unable to break it.

Lucy was so startled when he eventually moved that she shrank back with a soft cry of alarm, an action which drew his fleeting irritation. Her involuntary step backwards brought her up against the opposite wall, where she stayed, trying to appear as inconspicuous as possible. With luck he might forget she was there; he certainly appeared to have other things on his mind, and not happy ones if the grim expression on his taut face was anything to go by.

She watched warily as his head dropped forward to his chest in an attitude of frustration and despondency that some instinct told her were not emotions he gave in to often. Taking his head in his hands, he jammed his long, lean fingers into the dark waves that covered his head while releasing a string of violent and highly imaginative expletives.

The point came when she had had enough. 'Is that *really* necessary?' For some inexplicable reason she sounded like Miss Jones, her fourth-year form teacher, who had been known to make ultra-cool sixth-form boys cry like babies.

This man showed no inclination to weep. His head came up and his piercing eyes studied her with all the warmth of the jungle cat she had recently likened him to.

'Yes, it is!' he snarled.

'Well, if you don't mind, I'd be happier if you displayed a little more self-control.'

He looked at her as if he couldn't believe what he was

hearing. 'Oh, you would, would you? Well, I'd be a lot happier if you'd have kept your claws out of my brother.'

'Your brother?' she repeated blankly.

His head fell back, exposing the strong line of his brown throat. 'Dear God, I can't believe he could be this stupid—why couldn't he have waited? I'll kill him!' With an explosive motion the stranger with self-confessed homicidal tendencies straightened his shoulders, his laser-like gaze homing in once more on her alarmed face.

His expression was so accusing and inexplicably hostile that Lucy experienced an irrational need to defend herself; the problem was, she didn't have the faintest idea what she was meant to have done!

With equal abruptness the tension appeared to flow from his lean, loose-limbed frame. He released a long pent-up breath, causing his shoulders, which had been straining against the fabric of his shirt, to relax.

'No, he couldn't have, not yet, you're lying,' he stated confidently.

The fact he was correct didn't, in Lucy's opinion, lessen the insult. 'I am not lying!' Maybe once you had started doing so it was hard to stop?

The suggestion of an unpleasant smile in the intruder's deep-set, lustrously lashed eyes intensified as they locked down hard on to hers.

'In that case I'll wait for him.' The suggestion of a smile became a fully formed mocking grin as Lucy's eyes widened in dismay.

'Do you mind if I sit down?'

Lucy clenched her teeth, annoyed with herself for not having anticipated having her bluff being called.

'Yes, I do! Actually I'd mind very much,' Lucy cried, abandoning the cautious approach even though the possibility he was seriously unbalanced was seeming more likely with each passing second.

For the first time he seemed to notice the bronze figurine she had snatched up from the console table clutched in Lucy's raised hand. One dark brow lifted in sardonic question, his eyes slid back to her face.

CHAPTER TWO

DESPITE the fact her heart was banging against her ribcage and her knees were shaking, Lucy lifted her chin and returned the intruder's speculative stare defiantly.

'I'm quite prepared to use this,' she warned, drawing a deep, shuddering breath to fill her oxygen-depleted lungs.

Annie liked to term her flat in an expensive part of town *compact*; with this man in it, it felt more claustrophobic! Lucy's free hand nervously rubbed the smooth skin of her pale throat, causing red marks to spring up across the delicate skin.

His strongly defined sable brows lifted as their eyes clashed. 'I can see that,' he observed, a faint pucker of his brow betraying surprise.

His gaze was drawn to the determined set of her softly rounded chin and from there to the rapid rise and fall of her chest. Even without placing his hand over her heart—something he naturally had no intention of doing, though her breast would perfectly fit into the palm of his hand—he could almost feel the wild thud of her heartbeat.

A flicker of something close to admiration chased across his hard-edged face as it hit home that underneath the ice-cool façade Con's girlfriend was petrified and she'd come out fighting.

This set her apart from the Mias and Jasmines.

Connor's previous brides had been quite capable of stabbing anyone that got in their way in the back but the idea of either of those decorative ladies fronting someone this way was laughable. So she had guts—this didn't make her any less an unsuitable wife for his brother.

As he met her wide, slightly slanted eyes that were coloured the most unusual shade of warm amber he'd ever seen Finn experienced an inconvenient surge of guilt—the blonde might be the sort of woman he had no time for, but she hadn't set out to mess up his brother's life... Con didn't need any help. And Finn didn't get his kicks from scaring females for the fun of it.

'If you don't leave this second I'll call the police.' As she spoke Lucy surreptitiously edged a little closer to the telephone, still gripping the figurine.

'Listen, I didn't mean to frighten you...'

Lucy found herself staring at the hands spread palm upwards towards her, big, strong hands like the man himself, with long, tapering fingers...she pulled her gaze away as her stomach took another unscheduled dive. Lucy recognised the significance of the sensation with a jarring sense of panic.

Can you tell us what he was wearing? the police would ask. No, but she would be able to tell them all about his strong, sensitive hands! If that had been strictly true she would have felt less troubled. The fact was if called upon she could have given an extremely accurate description of this man, down to the faint white scar below his right eye.

If she had been like Annie, a person famed for her powers of observation, this would not have been anything to wonder at, but unlike her sister Lucy was not an observant person; she didn't notice the things you were meant to, like if a person was wearing a wedding ring, and the subtle differences between designer chic that cost a fortune and high-street cheap and cheerful were wasted on her.

She glared at the tall, effortlessly elegant figure and felt wretched that she'd been shallow enough to be impressed by the superficial package—no matter how good to look at it was!

'Well, naturally, knowing that makes me feel a *lot* better,' she snarled sarcastically.

Obviously she didn't appreciate the effort he was making to be nice. Finn would have laid money that she had never used that tone with Con—his brother might like aloof but he wasn't keen on caustic and that corrosive comment could have stripped paint.

'I'm quite harmless, you know.'

Which is more than can be said for you, sweetheart, he thought, his eyes drawn to the full, provocative, pouting line of her red lips. He suddenly felt less exasperated with his brother—it was easy to see why he'd fallen hard—women like Annie Foster, he brooded darkly, should carry a government health warning.

She almost choked as she heard this patently false claim. *Harmless!* Sure, harmless like a shark. She made herself take several calming breaths before she responded.

'And you expect me to take your word for that?' She wanted to make it quite clear to him that it was going to take a lot more than that to convince her it was safe to put aside her protection. To emphasise the point she hugged the heavy bronze firmly to her breast. 'For someone who *doesn't want to scare anyone* you have a funny way of going about it—pushing your way...'

'Listen, you can be as obstructive as you like, but I'm going to find him.'

Threats...it hadn't taken him very long to revert to type. Lucy felt a fleeting moment of sympathy for this person her visitor was pursuing with such grim tenacity—he was obviously not a man who made false promises.

She was pretty sure she wouldn't sleep nights if she

knew he was pursuing her. And maybe she'd sleep even less if he caught her...?

Now, *where did that come from*?

Deeply relieved he was blissfully unaware of the depraved depths her imagination had sunk to, she hurriedly removed her gaze from his mouth...an area which seemed to exert a deleterious influence on her imagination.

'*Him!* What him?' She demanded with an exasperated sigh. 'Listen, I've no idea who you are, or what you want, but I do know that if you don't leave I shall start screaming very loudly.'

It was crude and not actually a very effective threat but hopefully he didn't know that at this time of day all the neighbours were at work and even if she screamed her lungs out it was highly unlikely anyone would hear her.

His lip curled. 'Are you trying to tell me you don't know who I am?'

Lucy gave a little laugh. 'You're not a famous hairdresser, are you?'

His dark brows drew together in a straight line. 'Do I look like a hairdresser?'

Lucy's glance slid up the length of his well-muscled frame. 'I don't know. Maybe if you had a better haircut,' her lips twitched at the irresistible image that entered her head, 'and black leather trousers...'

'*What!*' He was looking at her as if she was certifiable, and small wonder.

Lucy's impish grin vanished as her features morphed into a more appropriate sombre expression.

'Well, the point is you could be anyone.' It was hard to point out anything with conviction while seeing his long limbs covered in tight black leather. If the result had been amusing and a little silly—like ninety-nine per cent of the male population similarly clad—it would have been less distracting.

But the raunchy image of brooding masculinity in her head was anything but *silly*! This was not the best time to discover a leather fetish.

'I said who I—'

'No,' she cut in firmly. 'You didn't. Cast your mind back,' she suggested before he could dispute what she'd said, 'and I think you'll find that actually you neglected the little niceties when you were pushing your way in uninvited, and don't bother enlightening me now,' she pleaded. 'I don't *care* who you are—I just want you to go...now!' She gestured firmly towards the door with the figurine. Pride impelled her to add, 'Oh, and just for the record, I'm not scared, I'm mad.'

'Relax, Ms Foster.' Lucy, who doubted she had ever felt less relaxed, glared at him. 'I'm Finn.'

It suited him.

Lucy's slender shoulders lifted and she shook her head. *'Finn?'*

A flicker of impatience crossed his handsome features. 'Finn Fitzgerald. I'm looking for Con. Where is he?'

'Con?' Then something in her dazed brain clicked: *Fitzgerald*. The same surname as Annie's boyfriend, it couldn't be a coincidence.

Finn saw the flash of recognition in her eyes and nodded.

'Con is my brother...for my sins.' With a weary gesture he thrust his hands into his trouser pockets. The action pulled the worn denim tight against his muscular thighs. 'Your boyfriend, the man who you're planning to marry.'

Lucy dragged her gaze back to his face, the flags of guilty colour fading with dramatic speed from her cheeks. Her eyes widened as his last comment finally sank in. Her mouth fell open in shock.

'*Marry?*' she squeaked. 'Did you say *marry*?'

She did a rapid mental calculation—heavens, give or take the odd day or two, Annie had only known this Con three weeks at the most! A sane person didn't commit themselves to a person for life after knowing them for a few weeks. In Lucy's book a sane person didn't commit themselves full stop, but she was prepared to acknowledge not everyone shared her extreme views.

She shook her head slowly from side to side. 'That can't be right. No, you must have got it wrong...'

'You mean he hasn't asked you yet?' Sounding insultingly relieved, Finn ignored her prohibition and pushed the magazines to one side before lowering his lean, rangy frame onto the sofa with a sigh. Lucy's indignation increased as he closed his eyes and burrowed his head into the soft leather headrest. 'That's something, I suppose,' he conceded with a yawn.

'Make yourself at home, why don't you?' she began tartly before she broke off, a thoughtful expression crossing her face. 'I take it you're not here to offer him—your brother—your congratulations?'

'What do you think?' he drawled without opening his eyes.

Lucy's eyes narrowed; she never had warmed to men who thought their opinions were the only ones that counted. 'So you're going to tell your...*Con* not to get married and he won't.' Lucy couldn't keep the scorn from her voice; if Connor Fitzgerald was that malleable then Annie was definitely well rid of him. 'It's that simple?'

'I wish it were.'

'Are you sure he's *definitely* going to ask?' Lucy still couldn't shake the suspicion that this was all a mistake, like him assuming she was Annie...she supposed she ought to explain about that... 'You know that for a fact?'

If he did? Her mind raced; Annie was normally incredibly sensible, and, focused on her career from early on, she had not had much time for romance. But then Lucy had never seen her talk about a man the way she spoke about Con Fitzgerald. Lucy uncomfortably recalled the soft glow in her sister's eyes when she'd spoken about the romantic weekend she was spending with him. Was it possible...? Was she besotted enough to say yes to this man's proposal without considering the consequences?

Oh, God...!

Lucy suddenly needed the support of a conveniently placed chair.

The heavy eyelids lifted and those disconcerting eyes scanned her face. Maybe his intervention hadn't been necessary after all; the blonde iceberg didn't look or sound as though a proposal was something she'd look on favourably. If this was the case it was his duty as a good brother to make sure things stayed that way.

'I couldn't say about today, but he certainly intended to when he emailed me last night...'

'You mean he's likely to have changed his mind by today?'

'Well, you know Con, he's a creature of impulse.'

The more she heard about this Con the less she liked the sound of him.

'But you must have thought he meant it or you wouldn't be here,' she reasoned.

He acknowledged her words with a shrug. 'Well, yes, he did sound convincing, which is why I flew straight back from the States...' He lifted his head and flexed his shoulders, rotating his neck to relieve tension tying his muscles in knots before closing his eyes once more.

Since the email in question Con had gone to ground, conveniently not responding to any of his own attempts to make contact. When Con was in love he wanted the whole world to be the same way, when he was happy he liked to share it. Finn could only assume he was regretting his impulsive candour.

'Your travel arrangements are really not my concern and neither is…'

Without warning the blue eyes lifted, bringing them into direct collision with her own, and Lucy's angry words dried as inexplicably the searing contact seemed to sever the link between her brain and vocal cords.

She wondered whether maybe he was picking up on something of what she was feeling because an odd expression washed over his severe features, making him appear for one split-second disconcerted.

Dragging a frustrated hand through his dark hair, he got to his feet in a fluid motion that caused Lucy's stomach muscles to tighten in a disturbing manner. 'Listen, just tell me where he is,' he suggested in a weary voice. 'You know you're going to so why prolong something neither of us is enjoying?'

He could say that again! 'Why do you assume I'm going to tell you? Did you fetch the thumbscrews?'

'Call this a war of attrition—I'm not moving until you tell me what I want to know.'

'I can't…' she began in exasperation. 'I…'

'I know—*you love him*,' came the blightingly cynical retort. '*Everyone* loves Con, sweetheart…he's a very lovable guy,' he pronounced with a sneer. 'But didn't his track record make you think that maybe it wasn't the best idea?'

'I don't love him—'

'Well, that makes things easier.'

'I wish it did.' Lucy's distracted gaze abruptly refocused on his face. '*Track record?*' That had an ominous sound to it.

As the fantastic topaz eyes looked back at him suspiciously Finn began to wonder how much she actually knew about his brother's history.

'Well, what else would you call two failed marriages?'

Lucy gulped. 'A track record,' she agreed quietly. 'He's divorced?' Annie, she thought grimly, had kept awfully quiet about that bit—always supposing she knew.

There was no doubt the blonde's shock was genuine, which surprised Finn, since his brother was not a secretive sort of guy; in fact he was transparently open. So much so that Finn had frequently squirmed to hear his sibling confiding his innermost feelings to almost total strangers. Why his brother felt the need to parade his emotional insecurities was almost as inexplicable to Finn as was the fact women appeared to find his supposed vulnerability irresistible.

'You did say *two failed marriages*?' Lucy repeated, forgetting to sound tough, calm and in control.

'Well, he got married twice. I'm assuming he got divorced both times.' Finn's lips twitched when his flip response drew a shock-horror gasp from the statuesque blonde, who gazed up at him with saucer-like Bambi eyes. He was beginning to suspect she had puritan tendencies; maybe that was the reason behind Con's untypical reticence?

Perhaps she was one of those types who pursued faces in the media—a fame groupie. Though a couple of appearances on local news programmes and a creditable performance in a documentary only gave Con the most tenuous claim to this sort of fame.

'You mean you don't know?' It seemed to Lucy that the elder Fitzgerald took the matrimonial state just as casually as his brother did.

Finn's eyes narrowed. 'Don't you?'

Lucy took a deep breath and, ignoring his searching

question, evaded the sweep of his narrowed eyes—she hardly dared ask the next question but decided it was best to know the worst straight off.

'Does he...does he have any children?' she whispered.

Finn's cold blue eyes swept over her face. It didn't require any special gifts to see his reply meant a lot to her—not only were her crossed fingers clearly on view but she also appeared to be holding her breath.

'So you wouldn't be attracted to a man who came with that sort of baggage...?'

'I thought the entire point about attraction was you don't have a choice about it.' The observation sent an inexplicable shiver down Lucy's spine.

'So marrying someone who'd had a child by someone else would not bother you...?' His expressive lips curled. *'Please...?'* he begged derisively.

Anger whipped through her. 'Why do I get the feeling I've been tested and found wanting? And without me giving an opinion on the subject too...how clever of you...'

'There's no need to be defensive,' he cut back, his jaw clenching. 'It wasn't a criticism.'

Like hell it wasn't!

'Whew, that's a weight off my mind.' In her estimation he was just about stupid and prejudiced enough to accept her dry retort at face value. 'For a minute there I thought you were suggesting I was so selfish, so immature that I wouldn't be able to cope with the man I loved having had a life before me...or that he might have other people with a call on his affections.' Without warning her eyes filled.

'And then there's the furniture issue,' she choked.

Finn didn't want to ask but had to. *'Furniture...?'*

'Kids with sticky fingers are just *hell* on the upholstery—the mess, that is, not the kids. Just for the record...' she wiped a hand across her eyes '...look what you've done, made me so mad I'm crying... God, is this stuff water-proof...?' Running mascara was all she needed.

Checking on the state of her make-up in the mirror, she didn't have the satisfaction of seeing that she had thoroughly disconcerted Finn, who was staring at her neat rear with an appreciative but perplexed expression.

'Resorting to tears if rational argument fails...'

Lucy spun around, her eyes flashing. 'You wouldn't know rational if it bit you on the bum!'

His lips quivered faintly '...Is a tried and tested method, but I must admit I didn't really think it was your style.'

'You'd know about my style...?'

'I don't know why you're being so aggro; I was simply admiring what I took to be your candour and realism. It's not easy to bring up a child when it's your own, but when it comes to someone else's... With the best will in the world you can't love a child who isn't your own the same way.'

Lucy held up her hand—if she had to listen to any more of this nonsense she would explode!

'I hate to interrupt your flow, but you haven't answered my question. Does your brother have a child? Oh, and incidentally I disagree with almost everything you just said,' she told him with a brilliant, brittle smile.

'Now, there's a surprise.'

'Violently,' she confirmed, ignoring his dry insert. 'I think you're spouting a lot of rubbish.'

'Don't hold back, will you?'

Lucy didn't. 'You don't have to look very far to see plenty of examples of people making terrific parents to children who are not genetically theirs,' she pointed out heatedly. 'A child needs love and security and I don't think it matters if the person who gives it gave birth to them. Now does your brother have children?'

There was a startled silence, interrupted only by the gentle hiss of her emotional hyperventilation.

'No, *he* doesn't.' There was a limit to how far he was prepared to blacken his brother's name in an attempt to make him a less attractive prospective groom.

Lucy released a relieved sigh, then looked puzzled. If there was no child, what had that been all about...? Then her sixth sense kicked in.

'But you do.' She didn't know why she had assumed he wasn't married. Men who looked like him usually were, unless they were gay, and his testosterone levels were definitely not in question.

'Con told you about Liam?'

Lucy shook her head. 'It was just the way you said...not that it's any of my business...' she added with an embarrassed shrug.

Annie was right—it was about time she stopped saying the first thing that came into her head.

'True.'

Lucy had thought his sneer couldn't get any more pronounced—she was wrong.

Her gold eyes narrowed. 'So what number marriage are you on?' Wearing a wedding ring ought, in Lucy's opinion, to be a legal requirement for men—especially ones that looked as unmarried as this one!

'I've never been married.' And he was sick to the back teeth of women who would have liked to alter that situation, women who thought they could claim a place in his heart by showing him what a perfect mother for Liam they would be.

Lucy didn't quite know how best to respond to his 'want to make something of it?' attitude.

'Neither, for the record, do I have a partner; there is just me and Liam.'

His attitude made it pretty clear he had no intention of altering that situation.

'What a pity,' she sighed. 'I only have the stamina to pursue one Fitzgerald boy at a time.' The man was obviously so full of himself that he thought that no woman could look at him without thinking wedding bells. She gave him an encouraging don't-give-up-hope smile. 'But I'm sure you'll find someone willing to overlook you being a single parent.' And a complete pain in the rear. 'So,' she added brightly, 'you find time to look after your son *and* play nursemaid to your brother…that's just so *amazing*…' But fairly normal behaviour for your average control freak.

Far from being thrown off balance by her sweet-tongued maliciousness, the victim of her vitriol was looking at her as if he hadn't seen her before…the speculative light of interest in his blue eyes made Lucy shift uncomfortably.

'Just how long have you two known one another?' Finn queried suspiciously.

The more time he spent in this woman's prickly company the less she seemed like the type to hold Con's interest— scare the wits out of him…now, that he *could* see. And, while it was just feasible that for reasons of his own Con might have kept her in the dark about his previous marriages, as one of the world's most hopelessly doting uncles he would never have kept quiet about Liam.

Something was going on here and he intended to find out what it was.

'I don't know him at all,' Lucy replied with an abstracted frown.

What was Annie thinking of, getting involved with someone who sounded as shallow and unstable as Con Fitzgerald…? Besides, if Annie did marry Connor that would make her related in a round-about way to Finn

Fitzgerald, who had a son, no wife and seemed to like it that way!

One brother was a serial groom, the other a misogynist. God, if Annie makes me a sister-in-law to that pair I might never forgive her. Combine the less disastrous qualities of each brother and you might have a halfway decent man, but separately a girl would have to be insane to get involved with the dysfunctional Fitzgerald clan.

'At least you're beginning to realise that.'

The unfamiliar note of warm approval in his voice made Lucy look up in surprise. Finn Fitzgerald was watching her closely—finding herself the focus of such blue-eyed intensity did not give her a warm feeling of security!

'Realise what?'

'An attraction often blinds you to the fact you are incompatible with the object of your desire...'

He lost her right there.

Object of desire! It was as if the words had clicked a switch in her head. The images that appeared were so shocking she let out a small, soundless gasp before clicking that switch in her head firmly into the off position.

'And even if you know deep down you pretend to yourself that the differences don't...' Finn frowned as he felt his argument losing coherence, a fact not unrelated to the fact the top button of her jacket had unfastened, revealing the lacy edge of the camisole she wore underneath and a hint of gentle creamy cleavage.

Lucy, who was confident she could have written a book on Finn Fitzgerald's faults, opened her mouth to tell him so when it occurred to her just in time that this would only be an appropriate argument if she was attracted to him—which she wasn't! Such an idea was ludicrous...laughable...preposterous... Her eyes followed the line of his throat which led inevitably to his strong, passionate mouth—oh, *God*…!

Lucy's jaw dropped, her mind went darkly blank with horror, so blank she didn't even register who she was sharing her wistful observation with—oh, Annie had definitely been right when she'd accused her of *opening your mouth first and thinking later*!

'Life would be much, much simpler if mindless sex was the best basis for a long-term relationship.'

Finn's imagination helpfully supplied a vivid visualisation of his only brother having head-banging sex with the blonde and a fist tightened in his belly.

The strangled sound focused Lucy's attention back to his lean, dark face. 'Did you say something?'

'Are you saying you don't feel anything for Con beyond basic lust?'

Under the circumstances his righteous indignation struck Lucy as more than a little perverse and she felt like telling him so—wasn't he the one who didn't *want* her to be in love with his brother…?

'Don't you approve of lust?' she asked innocently. She was pleased to see a flicker of annoyance move at the back of his eyes. 'You should try it, excellent sex can make you feel good after a really bad day.'

They definitely came from her mouth so there was no way she could dissociate herself from the provocative words. A person would be excused for thinking that she *wanted* to wind him up.

By the time his long-lashed eyes had shimmied over the entire length of her slender body Lucy was finding it hard to disguise the fact she was breathing as if she'd just run a marathon.

'I've had a really bad day.'

She didn't just hear the lazy purr of his voice, she *felt* it; it rippled through her entire body.

Taunting him no longer seemed daring or provocative, it just seemed plain stupid.

'The way *my* day is going, having the ceiling fall or the plumbing spring a leak would be an improvement and I'd prefer either scenario to sex with you!' Lucy was dismayed to hear a definite hint of desperation creeping into her defiant response.

'I'd like to take up the challenge, sweetheart, if only to discover if you do great sex or just talk great sex.'

Lucy's eyes widened in shocked dismay to hear her comments interpreted this way. 'It wasn't a challenge,' she denied, squirming with mortification that he might think... that he might think she...!

Finn watched the innocent act—it was a very good act—and his handsome face hardened. 'I've more important things on my mind. You may be playing, but my brother *believes* he loves you. When Con falls he really falls...'

'Good for him!' Lucy snapped, her skin cooling but not her temper. 'But does he have to marry *everyone* he falls for?' she demanded, her bosom swelling in indignation on Annie's behalf.

There was a startled silence and then a sound that sounded suspiciously like a laugh in Finn Fitzgerald's brown throat was almost immediately cut off as he explained. 'Con's got some pretty old-fashioned ideas, which wouldn't in themselves be such a problem if he wasn't fatally attracted to totally the wrong type of women.'

'Wrong type of women...?' Lucy looked down at herself arrayed in the beautiful borrowed suit. 'You're saying that An...*I'm* the wrong type of woman?' She wasn't taking his comments personally, she told herself, she was just feeling justifiably indignant on behalf of her sister, who in her opinion any man would be damned lucky to get.

'Con might come over as a modern guy, but don't be fooled...' he warned.

'There's no chance of that,' Lucy promised grimly.

In her view modern man was a myth—scrape the surface of the most politically correct of men and you would discover an old-fashioned chauvinist...of course, with some men you didn't have to scrape at all and Finn Fitzgerald was indisputably one of that number. The man had political incorrectness off to an art form.

'Basically Con needs to be the most important thing in his woman's life...'

A family trait, no doubt. 'Him and just about very other man ever to draw breath,' she murmured acidly.

'He is never going to be happy with a woman who will schedule him some time between her meetings. He needs someone soft, warm and generous, not a hard-nosed ball-breaker.'

A gurgling sound escaped Lucy's clamped lips, and it was several seconds before she could trust herself to speak.

'Are you calling *me* a ball-breaker?' she asked in a dangerously soft voice.

Head tilted slightly to one side, he regarded her with that twisted cynical smile which Lucy was beginning to think was the norm for him.

'Well, from the look of you, you're not likely to trade in your wardrobe of designer suits for a baby, are you?'

A woman displayed ambition, had a modicum of success and she was automatically as hard as nails—*talk about stereotyping*! 'Leaving aside the fact my maternal instincts or lack of them are none of your business—'

'Listen,' he interrupted impatiently, 'I'm the one who Con will turn to when you've finished him so that makes it my business. We run a business together and the last divorce left him incapable of getting out of bed in the morning let alone coming into the office.'

Lucy released a scornful laugh and planted her hands squarely on her slender hips. 'And here was I, thinking your offensive attitude at least stemmed from a genuine, though misplaced, concern for your brother, but I see now it's just your profit margins you're worried about. I suppose if Connor loses the plot you're in serious trouble.'

According to Annie the incredible success of the Irish-based software company owed everything to Connor Fitzgerald's brilliance. In fact until now Lucy hadn't even realised that there was a brother involved. She only considered the possibility that her sister's take on the situation might be slightly biased for a moment before dismissing it.

'What do you do?'

Finn, used to hearing himself referred to as the dynamic inspiration behind one of the most successful software set-ups on record, blinked to hear himself designated a hanger-on.

'Some people think I'm quite good with figures,' he responded mildly. Those people included the ones who wrote column after admiring column in respected financial journals about his charismatic leadership and technical knowledge to match.

'You don't look like an accountant,' Lucy sniffed, disgruntled he'd not responded to her jibe.

'Aren't you guilty of stereotyping?'

This suggestion reduced Lucy to a state of speechless incredulity that lasted several seconds. *'Me…?'* she choked. 'My God, but you've got a nerve!'

'It comes in handy when I'm adding a particularly hostile column of figures.'

Lucy judged the innocent look he was wearing to be extremely unconvincing.

'Did I give you the impression I'm even slightly interested in what you do? Sorry about that.'

He sighed. 'It's always the same—women find out what I do and they switch off. I've often wondered about trying something a bit more glamorous.'

'I'd say you've already exhausted this particular line of irony. I'm quite prepared to accept I'm in the presence of talent, so can we return to the actual subject of this conversation…namely your brother?'

'By all means.'

'So what you're saying is he needs a woman who puts her own life on hold to become a homemaker, who produces babies and bakes bread when she's not massaging her husband's ego?' she inserted, returning to the original theme.

'The bread-making is optional…but basically, yes, I think that sort of woman would suit Con very well,' he agreed, seemingly oblivious to the sarcasm in her voice.

'Suddenly I'm not surprised he's been divorced twice already,' she choked, quivering with outrage. 'But are you *quite* sure you're not guilty of assuming your brother's needs are the same as your own? I can see *you're* a classic case of arrested development, but isn't it just possible that *he's* moved beyond the Neanderthal?'

Lucy's initial satisfaction at seeing him react angrily to her attack only lasted until she realised that all she'd succeeded in doing with her smart-mouth tactics was drag this thing out—he wasn't the type not to retaliate.

And retaliate he did, but not in the manner she had anticipated.

'My *needs*?' he drawled, rolling the word around his tongue.

The way he said *needs* sent a sharp stab of sizzling sexual awareness through Lucy's unprepared body, which was, of course, just what he'd intended; he used his sexuality like a weapon to confuse and disable the enemy—confusion was the least of her problems.

It was worse somehow that his expression was hidden from her by the sweep of his long lashes that cast a sinister shadow across his sharp cheekbones, because that gave her imagination freedom to be inventive and it rose to the occasion.

She had arranged her features in a studied pose of indifference by the time his attention returned to her face. Despite her efforts she had the creepy impression he knew exactly how she was feeling.

'My *needs* don't include marriage.' The faint intonation again gave her a shivery feeling and his uninterested shrug was a calculated slap in the face.

She hated Finn Fitzgerald.

'Neither do mine.'

'They all say that.'

Lucy held on to her temper—it wasn't easy.

Did he think that all women's aim in life was to hook a husband? Wake up, this is the twenty-first century! Women have a choice these days, she wanted to yell at him. They could choose to go down the marriage-and-babies route if that was what they wanted, or enjoy uncomplicated sex, or even, like herself, duck out of the entire messy game. She didn't even miss it…what was there to miss? Sex had been nice but nothing extra-special…though she did miss the hugs and kissing; she liked kissing… Her speculative gaze brushed across Finn Fitzgerald's mouth; he would be a good kisser.

The direction of her thoughts brought a prickle of heat that spread like a rash across her body.

'This one means it, but chin up, I'm sure there will be lots of women out there, some of them not even on medication, whose lives will be blighted by that news.'

A reluctant laugh was wrenched from his throat. 'You have a very smart mouth.' Not to mention a kissable one.

'Thank you.' Lucy frowned in concentration. 'So what you're saying is that *I* should concentrate my efforts on Connor…?' she asked, pouting innocently up at him.

'No,' he growled, 'you should not!'

Her nostrils quivered as she glared at him with distaste— he thought she was serious. 'I've only just realised that I'm talking to a genuine unreconstructed chauvinist.'

'I don't consider myself a chauvinist.'

'They never do. I suppose this perfect bride for your brother would be a virgin too?'

'Let's be realistic here…unless you're trying to tell me you're a virgin,' he suggested with a scorn that made Lucy's teeth clench.

'No, I'm not, but Annie is…was…' Lucy stopped…just how far had Annie's relationship with Connor gone…? Had she…? 'Oh, my God, this is awful…!' Concern for her sister, who, despite her high-powered career and sophisticated manner, was actually a world-class romantic idealist, made her voice shrill as she advanced towards the tall figure. 'You have to do something; Annie can't marry your brother!'

It was only when he picked the figurine from her fingers and looked pointedly down at his chest that Lucy realised she had grabbed handfuls of Finn Fitzgerald's shirt in her free hand.

'Sorry,' she murmured gruffly. While she awkwardly patted down the crumbled fabric some corner of her mind registered the hard and inflexible as in solid-steel nature of the chest her fingers smoothed the cloth over. 'Sorry…'

'You're not Annie Foster…?'

His inability to grasp the obvious made Lucy lose the last of her unravelling patience. 'My, you are fast; of *course* I'm not Annie,' she announced witheringly. 'Did I say I was Annie…?'

A nerve began to pulse in his lean cheek as their unfriendly glances locked tight. 'You didn't say you *weren't,*' he pointed out grimly.

'So you just *assumed* I was the sort of woman who would marry a man I hardly know…?'

'You were what I expected to find,' Finn retorted in his own defence.

'Which was…?'

His eyes slid from hers. 'Let's just say you look like the type Con goes for.' When she opened her mouth that altered.

Lucy's generous lips pursed. 'Isn't it a tad late to be concerned about offending me? Be frank—I can take it.'

'Fine.' He shrugged his broad shoulders. 'If you must know, my brother goes for hard-as-nails bottle-blondes with flat chests and long legs.'

Lucy gave a gasp of incredulous fury and her much-maligned bosom heaved.

Finn shrugged. 'You have all the credentials,' he observed simply.

CHAPTER THREE

LUCY lifted a hand to her silvery fair head. 'I'm a natural blonde!' Like that was the worst thing he said about me, she thought.

He waited until the heat she felt travel up her neck had encompassed her entire face in a fiery glow before responding in a slow maddening drawl.

'Sure you are.'

It took several moments for Lucy, who had always considered herself a placid, even-tempered sort of person, to control the urge that made her want to wipe that smug, superior sneer off his face. As she thought a little more about it she discovered there was a certain novelty value for someone who had frequently heard herself stigmatised by friends as *too soft for her own good* to suddenly hear herself declared as hard as *nails*.

'Maybe I do have all the *qualifications*,' she conceded with her best hard bitch I-don't-give-a-damn shrug. 'But Annie doesn't.'

She promptly spoilt this heartless impression by almost immediately slipping out of character. Her soft lips began quivering the moment she lifted up the gilt-framed photo from the sideboard. Catching her full lower lip between her teeth, she turned her head to one side to hide the fact her eyes had filled with tears. With an angry sniff she waved it at him.

'*Annie* is an emotional redhead,' she told him thickly as she jabbed a triumphant finger at the flaming curls on top of her smiling sister's head.

42

'You seem to have the emotional part in common,' Finn observed drily as the iceberg, golden tear-drenched eyes glittering, glared at him in a frankly murderous fashion.

He couldn't help but notice—in a *strictly* objective sort of way—that as she simmered in a very un-iceberg manner the angry animation in her face dramatically improved her bland good looks.

'Do you know the tip of your nose has turned pink?'

Lucy lifted a hand to the offending item then, frowning darkly, let it fall away. 'You are the most unpleasant man I've ever met.'

'Are you always so inclined to dramatise?' he asked with interest.

'I am *not* inclined to dramatise, and Annie,' Lucy continued in an angry, shaking voice, 'just for the record, wears a D cup. So maybe you don't know your brother's tastes quite as well as you thought,' she jeered.

He didn't look at the photo, which pictured a smiling Annie looking nothing remotely like the stereotype he'd so scathingly described. Not that she was surprised; this was exactly what she would have expected of someone who was clearly congenitally incapable of accepting he could be wrong about anything.

So blondie was loyal and she wasn't sleeping with his brother.

Finn experienced a strong wave of relief which he concluded had to be connected to the fact he was no longer faced with the task of convincing his brother he wasn't in love with a woman who even he, who didn't possess Con's weakness for blondes, could recognise was extremely...? The line bisecting his dark brows deepened fractionally as he tried to analyse the indefinable something about this female he knew spelt trouble.

Finn gave up trying to define the indefinable but felt

deeply sorry for the man fool enough to allow her to get under his skin. He caught a glimpse of the photo as she was replacing it and did a double take.

'That's *you?*'

As he spoke Finn's eyes were not on the redhead but on the barefooted figure standing beside her on a wide stretch of windswept beach. Technically the photo wouldn't have won any prizes but he wasn't looking at composition or lighting, he was looking at her smiling mouth…you just *knew* that those slightly parted pink lips would have tasted of salt. He found himself wondering if the person taking the photo had kissed the salty film off—he would have been tempted to if he had been there.

'Yes.' She bit her tongue to stop herself babbling an apologetic explanation that, unlike Annie, who was extremely photogenic, she didn't actually take a particularly good picture…as if it mattered that he saw her looking like a scarecrow.

She watched with an uneasy frown as the tall figure bent closer to get a better look. Now she didn't want him to look at it he was interested—this perversity seemed to Lucy to typify the actions of the wretched man who obviously had awkwardness off to a fine art.

Maybe the best way to get rid of him was to beg him to move in? Better not…with her luck he'd think she meant it!

Finn's expression grew frankly incredulous as he looked from the blonde dressed in a pair of cut-off jeans and skimpy T-shirt pushing her tousled, windblown hair off her lightly freckled nose as she squinted back at the camera to the statuesque creature with the sleek hair and flawless porcelain skin standing beside him in a suit that had 'designer' written all over it.

'I don't believe it,' he said, looking back at the girl with the freckles and smile with a shake of his head.

He reached for the photo to get a better look, but Lucy beat him to it and, whipping the frame from under his nose, pressed it to her bosom.

'I'm not about to undergo DNA testing to satisfy you.' She determined not to look at her reflection in the mirror even though the way his glance kept returning critically to her mouth made her suspect her lipstick had smudged. 'I am exactly who I said I was. What reason,' she demanded hotly, 'would I have for lying?'

'That's the point, isn't it. You didn't say who you were,' he growled belligerently. 'You just let me...'

'Prattle on?' Lucy planted her hands on her hips and regarded him with growing resentment.

'*Prattle...?*'

'Possibly,' she suggested loftily, ignoring his stunned echo, 'I didn't say who I was because you didn't give me a chance to say anything. You were too busy pushing your way in uninvited and throwing insults at me.'

Finn dismissed this suggestion with an imperious shake of his dark, shapely head. 'And just what am I supposed to call you if you're not Con's girlfriend?'

Lucy could surmise from his tone and attitude pretty much what he'd have liked to call her—she was just surprised he hadn't; nothing so far about his behaviour had suggested he was squeamish about insulting her! Taking a deep breath, she lifted her chin to a combative angle.

She gave a thin, goaded smile. 'I'm a flat-chested, emotionally inadequate, *natural* blonde.' The resentful words were wished unsaid almost before she'd finished enumerating the insults he'd heaped upon her.

The very last thing she needed was him walking away

with the idea she gave a damn what he thought about her. He was insufferable enough without that!

She took a calming breath. 'I'm Lucy Foster.'

'*Foster...?* Her sister?'

Lucy nodded.

A sound of impatience escaped from between his clenched even white teeth. 'I still don't understand why the hell you didn't say so instead of wasting time...!' His eyes narrowed. 'Unless that was your intention?'

'I'm part of the plot now?' Lucy was beginning to see how this man's twisted mind worked. 'I was giving the lovers time to give you the slip.' She shook her head. 'Have you *always* been this paranoid?'

'Listen, sweetheart, we're on the same side here.'

Lucy folded her arms across her chest and released an incredulous laugh. 'How do you work that one out?' This one should be good.

'Do you want your sister to marry Con?'

His blunt question managed to wipe the smug smile from Lucy's face, but her response was limited by her unfortunate inability to lie convincingly and her extreme reluctance to admit she agreed with him—about anything!

'I think my sister is a million times too good for your brother, but Annie is an adult and quite capable of making her own decisions...' And her own mistakes she thought gloomily.

He listened to her cautious response, not bothering to disguise his scepticism. 'And you think getting married to someone you hardly know is a good decision?'

There was a short pause before Lucy replied in a tight, goaded voice, 'It doesn't matter what I think.'

His cold eyes swept across her face measuringly. 'In other words you hate the idea of it just as much as I do.'

She was alarmed to find that without actually appearing

to move his body had curved in an intimate fashion towards her. She blinked warily as an unfamiliar glint appeared in his blue eyes, which had so far been by turn hotly furious and icily contemptuous.

Lucy felt her breath quicken and would have stepped back had not the backs of her thighs already been pressed against a coffee-table. She was trying so hard to act as if nothing was happening—as if her heart wasn't hammering and there wasn't a warm, sinking feeling low in her belly—that her awareness of him as an incredibly attractive male hurt, it physically hurt.

Her tongue wasn't the only thing that acted independently of her brain around this man!

'You know, I think we should work together on this.'

Lucy had been on the receiving end of Finn Fitzgerald's contempt and nasty temper, but this was her first taste of his charm...and she found it infinitely more disturbing! He had the ability to look at a woman and make her feel as if she was the most important person in the world to him. Add a voice—*she knew all about that voice*—that could make a shopping list sound like an indecent proposal and you had a very dangerous proposition!

Knowing he'd probably successfully used this cynical method of getting his own way a million times before didn't prevent the hormonal rush—Lucy felt deeply ashamed of her body's weak response. If Con Fitzgerald possessed a voice with a fraction of the seductive power of his brother's she was hardly surprised Annie had decided he was the man she'd been saving herself for.

Making damned sure her wayward imagination didn't take any poetic licence interpreting the *working together* thing, she allowed her eyes to rest significantly on the strong hands that had come to rest on her shoulders.

With a wry look Finn immediately lifted them and took

a step back. 'I'm afraid I'm just a naturally tactile sort of guy.'

Lucy gulped as the muscles low across her abdomen tightened in a rippling sensation; this was information that she really didn't need to have in her possession.

'How nice for you, but I'd be grateful if you'd keep your touchy-feely side under control around me.'

From the way he was looking at her Lucy had the uncomfortable suspicion that he had a pretty accurate idea why the idea of being touched by him had her so spooked.

'I take it that *working together* was your idea of a joke?' she croaked. Peculiarly Lucy could still feel the weight of his hands, the warm imprint of his long fingers where they had lain. No mystery about that, Luce, you fancy the pants off him...

'Con is with your sister; presumably you know where they are?'

So this was the reason for the charm offensive—he wanted her to lead him to the couple.

'If I did I wouldn't tell you. Do you think I'd let you ruin my sister's life?' If what Annie wanted was the awful Connor then Lucy had every intention of making sure nobody messed it up for her.

'For God's sake, woman, can't you put aside your unreasonable dislike of me?'

Was he for real...? 'There's nothing *unreasonable* about it!' she interjected forcibly.

'I was feeling pretty unloved,' he admitted with a lazy smile. 'But I'm beginning to realise it's your way of showing affection.'

'I've met some men who were full of themselves,' she choked incredulously. 'But you,' she promised, 'are in a class of your own!'

'Thank you.'

The attractive flush of angry colour in her face condensed into two angry solid blocks of bright pink on her cheeks. 'Actually,' she hissed, 'my antagonism is a defence mechanism to hide the fact I'm secretly lusting after your body,' she sniffed sarcastically.

'I thought as much.'

'My God, what a piece of work you are! Do you *really* think all you have to do is flutter your lashes and I'll tell you what you want? I can't see what difference it will make if you do find your brother...or does he always do what his big brother tells him?' she wondered with a display of wide-eyed innocence.

Finn's smile faded and his incredibly handsome face darkened with displeasure. 'Of course he doesn't,' he snapped impatiently at the scornful suggestion.

'I'm curious—does he have to produce his girlfriends for the Finn Fitzgerald seal of approval?' She shook her head. 'I really think that you should get a hold of your control-freak tendencies and leave your brother to make his own mistakes,' Lucy advised briskly.

She had the unexpected pleasure of seeing that masterful square jaw of his actually sag for a brief moment as he received her advice with an expression of total, almost comical shock that lasted a full thirty seconds.

The expression that replaced it sent a shiver of apprehension up Lucy's rigid spine as did the smile that said he'd take great pleasure from making her eat her words.

'You're saying I'm a control freak?' he said in a casually conversational tone that was in stark contrast to the retributional gleam in his spectacular eyes.

'I speak as I find,' she revealed carelessly.

His eyelids dropped lazily but the gleam in the blue depths they concealed was anything but. 'And you find me...?' he prompted grimly.

'A bit hysterical.' And as her eyes locked with his the room tilted slightly.

There was a sibilant hiss as his breath whistled through his clenched teeth. 'So you're not worried...no nagging doubts...?'

She couldn't prevent the flicker of uncertainty that chased across her worried face. 'Well, I've only your word for it that they are planning to get married,' she countered crossly.

'If you're not sure, ring your sister and ask her.' His eyes narrowed. 'I take it you do have her number? Or, aha, I know—'

'Actually Annie left her mobile behind...' Her perfect make-up long forgotten, she screwed up her nose as her face assumed a tight mask of dislike. 'What do you mean, *Aha*...? I only spoke to Annie a little earlier, and I sort of think she'd have mentioned if she had any plans to get married in the near future.'

'If you say so.'

'I do say so.'

'You and your sister have no secrets?'

'Not about important things.' If he hadn't turned up, she thought, eyeing his disgustingly perfect profile resentfully, she'd still be in a state of blissful ignorance...relaxed and content if you discounted the interview nerves...

Oh, my God, the interview!

Her hand flew to her mouth and her eyes to the watch on her slender wrist.

'I'm going to be late!' she wailed. 'And it's all *your* fault,' she added, throwing Finn a venomous look before she lunged for the businesslike leather briefcase that Annie had insisted she borrow.

'Late for what?'

At that moment the phone rang. Thinking there was some

conspiracy at work to make her late for the interview, Lucy lifted the receiver.

'Hello,' she said in a not particularly friendly voice.

'What are you still doing there?' she heard her sister's voice demand. 'She's wimped out, Con...I was right—she's still there... Of course there won't be a perfectly good explanation. She's wimping out.'

Lucy turned her back on Finn and nursed the phone tight against her ear. 'I'm not wimping out, I'm just leaving,' she responded in a soft undertone.

'Speak up, I can't hear you.'

'I said I was just leaving.'

'Well, make sure you do.'

'Is that your sister?'

Lucy pressed her hand to the voice piece and turned around, her expression composed. 'No, it is not my sister; now, do you mind, this is a private conversation?'

'You won't mind if I just check on that, will you?' he murmured, advancing with purpose towards her.

'Yes I will!' she cried, hugging the phone to her middle and turning her back on him.

She felt his hand on her shoulder and panicked.

'Let me go!' she screeched a few moments later.

'I'm not doing the holding—you are!' Finn protested, releasing a grunt as she planted a fist in the centre of his chest.

Lucy opened her eyes and saw that he was telling the truth; Finn's hands were hanging loosely at his sides—her confinement had been a product of her imagination. 'What are you trying to do?' he rasped, catching her arm to steady her as she lost her balance.

Anything but touch you!

Lucy closed her eyes as her face was pressed into the

solid wall of his chest. Her nostrils flared as her senses were assailed by the warm, musky, masculine scent of his body.

Gasping for breath, she stepped away, feeling desperately embarrassed. Somehow in the brief and undignified tussle she had managed to overturn a small occasional table and a geranium in a pot had been smashed by the phone as it sailed to the other side of the room.

'You bit me,' Finn said, staring at the marks on his wrist.

He held out his arm so that Lucy could see the damage he referred to.

'I scratched you,' she corrected, her expression an uncomfortable mixture of shame and embarrassment, '*accidentally,*' she emphasised. 'It's these wretched nails.' They were going, she thought, looking with distaste at the red talons responsible for the damage. 'Besides, you were the one that started it, you big bully.' It did occur to her that he had actually emerged from the encounter looking more dishevelled than she was. 'I was just defending myself,' she contended stubbornly.

'Against what? I didn't lay a finger on you and you went psycho on me!'

Reviewing the blur of events, Lucy was becoming uncomfortably aware that his version bore more of a resemblance to what had actually happened than her own.

'If that's how you react when you don't want to share the phone I dread to think what you'd be like if you were defending something really important.'

Lucy straightened the lamp and didn't look at him. She walked over to where the phone lay half under a table and hitched the restricting pencil skirt of the slimline black suit above her knees—all thought of maintaining an elegant image long gone—before kneeling down on the carpet to retrieve it.

She lifted the receiver to her ear. 'It's dead.' Annie probably thinks I cut her off deliberately, she thought.

'I'm assuming that was the real Annie.'

Lucy lifted her head and discovered his eyes were on her thighs not her face. With a snort she pulled down the hem of her skirt. 'You're totally disgusting!' Was there some deeply buried part of her that *liked* disgusting...?

Finn appeared totally unfazed by her scathing comment. 'Sunk in depravity,' he agreed, fixing her with a narrow-eyed stare. 'Are you going to tell me where they are?'

'They're in a hotel in the Lake District; there, now you know as much as me.'

He subjected her to a moment of searching scrutiny before lifting one dark brow in a gesture that seemed to indicate he had finally accepted she was telling the truth.

Great, maybe he'd go now.

'If you dialled one-four-seven-one...'

Lucy gritted her teeth and firmly shook her head. Fully anticipating a battle of wills, she was surprised he accepted her refusal with a careless shrug of his magnificent shoulders.

'What's this?'

Lucy's eyes widened with dismay when she saw that he was holding the first chapter of her unfinished novel that she'd left lying on the sofa.

'Give that to me!' she cried, lurching to her feet with her hand outstretched. 'It's private.'

'This is a manuscript,' he discovered, flicking through the pages.

'*My* manuscript,' she gritted, snatching it from his hands.

'No violence, please,' he implored, holding up his hands. His unkind smile widened as she backed off, flushing. 'You're writing a book?'

'You find that amusing…?' This was *exactly* the reason she hadn't told anyone of her efforts to put the story that had been going around in her head on paper. Nobody took you seriously…if she was honest she didn't do so herself half the time.

'What's it about?'

'You wouldn't be interested.'

'Try me.'

Lucy gave an exasperated sigh. 'Fine…it's a coming-of-age story. Of an adolescent girl. Happy now?'

'Autobiographical?'

'Not even slightly,' she denied quickly.

'Have you got a publishing deal…?'

'I've only done the first chapter.'

'And how long have you been working on it?'

Only a stupendously insensitive person wouldn't have seen she didn't want to discuss the subject. 'I started it a few years ago but this is the first time I've worked on it for some time. Now, if you don't mind I have to be going.' She sifted through a pile of envelopes to find the one she'd scribbled down the address of her interview on.

The doorbell rang and Lucy groaned. 'Annie is never going to forgive me if I roll up late for this interview.'

'I'll get the door if you like,' he offered unexpectedly.

Lucy glanced up just as he was elegantly unfolding his long, lean length off the wall where he'd been leaning. She was too intent on the urgent necessity of finding that darned address to refuse, let him make himself useful, she decided, giving a quick affirmative nod. Given the circumstances she could only marvel at the man's capacity to act as though he was a welcome guest. He'd be offering to make tea next.

As she continued her feverish search she was aware of the sound of voices; Finn's deep, vibrant tones were easily distinguishable though she couldn't make out what was actually being said. The voices stopped and she heard the sound of the door closing just at precisely the moment she discovered what she'd been frenziedly searching for; with a sigh of relief she separated it from the pile of junk mail.

She sensed Finn enter the room. 'I really do have to be going now…' Lucy lifted her head and saw two uniformed policemen enter the room behind Finn.

She froze, fear pumping around her body. 'Oh, God!' she gasped. 'What's wrong…what's happened? Is it Annie or Mum—has there been an accident? Don't tell me to sit down, I don't want to sit down, and I hate sugar in tea, just tell me…'

Anxious words flowed seamlessly and incoherently from her lips and the uniformed figures on the receiving end of the high-pitched verbal assault looked taken aback.

It was Finn who put a soothing hand on her arm and stilled the flood.

'Nothing has happened; it's you they're worried about.'

Lucy shook her head, looking from him to the policemen. 'Me…! Don't be silly, why should they be worried about me?'

Finn flicked a dry look in the uniformed figures' direction and a thin, unamused smile formed on his lips. 'I think I'll let them explain that.'

'A Miss—er—' the thick-set officer consulted his notebook '—Anne Foster, the leaseholder of this property, I believe…?' Lucy nodded, her mind a total blur of bewilderment. 'Miss Foster reported a violent disturbance was taking place here; she thought there was an intruder.'

Lucy lifted a hand to her lips, her eyes wide as she realised what must have happened. 'The phone…I was on the phone when we…' Poor Annie at the other end must have assumed she was being attacked. God, she must be worried sick.

'Are you all right, miss?'

She looked up and saw that although the officer was speaking to her his suspicious glance was fixed on Finn, whose rigid attitude was clearly not soothing the other man's suspicions.

She knew he looked like an explosion waiting to happen because the idea of being considered a man who would raise a hand to a woman insulted him in the worst way possible, but the policeman didn't. She didn't pause to tackle the thorny issue of why she was suddenly such an authority on someone she had known for two minutes; instead, at a time when she might have taken pleasure from his discomfort, she experienced a strong surge of sympathy for his plight.

'Of course I'm all right.'

She saw the younger officer look at the upturned table and felt a guilty blush spread across her face.

'My sister was mistaken; there isn't a problem.'

'If you'd prefer to speak to us alone…' the older man suggested with a significant look in Finn's direction.

A strangled sound escaped Finn's throat and Lucy cut in firmly—now that the initial shock had worn off she was actually starting to feel quite indignant that anyone would think she was victim material.

'There is no violence domestic or otherwise here…he's not my boyfriend…in fact, I hardly know him. I don't even *like* him…!' she explained earnestly. 'Sorry,' she added with an apologetic grimace in Finn's direction, 'but I don't.'

Finn, who no longer looked nearly so tense, received this information like someone who could happily live without her liking him.

Lucy shot a narrowed stare at the younger police officer,

whose bout of coughing had started off sounding suspiciously like a laugh.

'Right, miss,' the older man said. 'You do understand we have to check out these sorts of reports.'

'Of course,' Lucy conceded graciously.

'You will let your sister know you are all right?'

'As soon as you're all gone,' she promised. 'Finn was just leaving. Weren't you, Finn?' She sent a sweet smile in his direction. 'Sorry to hurry you but I'm late for an interview.'

'What do you do?' the younger officer asked.

'The job is for a PA to the CEO.'

'Good luck, miss. Sir...' The policeman stood aside to let Finn pass through the door before him.

CHAPTER FOUR

THEY were really very understanding about her being late. The interview itself turned out to be not nearly as scary as Lucy had expected and they said loads of complimentary things about her before they came out with the inevitable *sorry but*…on this occasion…blah…blah…

Lucy walked out of the building, smiled at the pretty receptionist, who probably had a PhD in astrophysics, and exited via the glass swing doors into the sunshine. When she stopped to analyse her feelings she was surprised to discover the by far most significant one to surface was relief. Considering the trouble Annie had gone to to get her the interview, she felt rather ashamed of this reaction.

As she selected the quickest route to the nearest tube she began to wonder if a bus might not be quicker. All thoughts of the relative merits of the rail versus road left her head when the shadow of a tall figure fell across her path.

She knew without looking who it was and when the figure smoothly fell into step beside her Lucy's own stride lost its rhythm and she stumbled.

'How did you find me?' The man just didn't give up.

'I followed you,' he admitted, displaying no shame for his tactics. 'I made the cabbie's day when I said *follow that taxi*,' he recalled.

'Stalking is a criminal offence, and I know some nice policemen…' A sudden spasm of amusement crossed her face. 'Your face…' she recalled, gulping. 'It was…' A gurgle of laughter welled in her throat.

Finn gave a pained grimace. 'I must admit the humour of the situation passes me by just at this moment.'

'You should learn to laugh at yourself,' she advised kindly.

'I'll keep that in mind,' he promised, smiling thinly. 'Did you manage to let your sister know that you're all right?'

'I wondered how long the foreplay would last…thirty seconds, well done.'

'Thirty seconds…' His earthy laugh attracted the interested glances of several passers-by—actually even when he didn't laugh that happened. Lucy was discovering it was hard to be anonymous when you were walking beside Finn Fitzgerald. Could he *really* be as oblivious to the attention he drew…? 'Maybe *you* should learn to set your sights a little higher. Or start mixing with a more giving kind of guy.'

'You're a very crude and coarse man…' she choked, blushing deeply.

'It could be worse; I could be your boyfriend and you could *like* me…'

This amused reminder of her attempt to convince the police that she was not a victim made her flush deepen. 'I'm beginning to wish I'd let them drag you off in handcuffs,' she gritted. 'And for the record I'm not interested in *guys*.'

His mobile brows lifted. 'Now, *that* does surprise me…' he admitted frankly.

'I didn't mean *that*.'

'I know. I just couldn't resist winding you up, but the novelty is wearing off. There's no sport in something that's as easy as taking candy from a baby.' Still using the same light, bantering tone, he smoothly changed the subject. 'And how did Annie take the news I'd been visiting?'

Lucy's expression instantly grew defensive. 'She didn't—I didn't tell her.'

'Figures…' he drawled, sounding not particularly fazed by the news. 'Then how did you explain away the world war she overheard…?'

'I said the cat knocked a plant over and I fell over trying to catch it.'

'I think you're wise to keep it simple.'

'So glad you approve.'

'Did marriage happen to come into the conversation?'

'Well, I didn't mention it and neither did she. To be honest I think you're just being paranoid.' She shared her unfriendly glare between Finn and the stilettos that made her ankles and calves look marvellous but were clearly designed with torture in mind.

Why women voluntarily put themselves through such agony for the sake of a few admiring glances was beyond her.

'I've had enough of this.' Her abrupt declaration brought Finn's enquiring gaze to her determined face. Meeting his eyes—the brief collision was a signal for her pulse to quicken—she placed her hand on his forearm. Steel would have had more give, but it wouldn't have been warm.

Focus, Lucy! The muscular development of his body was irrelevant.

'Stay still!' Her abrupt words were accompanied by an imperious little gesture. Rather to her surprise Finn obeyed her abrupt command.

Steadying herself, Lucy bent down and slipped off the heels. The idea that she was touching him just to prove she could do so and feel nothing was clearly ludicrous.

She hooked the sling-backs over her finger and wriggled her toes. A sigh of voluptuous pleasure escaped her parted lips. The good part was being able to walk without fear of falling flat on her face; the bad part was the fact that the loss of the few vital inches meant she now barely topped Finn's shoulder. Though she doubted being a head shorter would have lessened his air of superiority, it was an integral part of him, like the colour of his eyes.

'Thanks,' she said, lifting her hand from his arm.

Now, was that so difficult? She felt like laughing at her fears; after all that soul searching she had made contact, quite literally, with the enemy and emerged virtually un-scathed, barring the vague tingling feeling in her fingertips.

It just went to show a person could exaggerate something out of all proportion; no, it was better by far to face your devils—they were inevitably less frightening than you imagined.

Now that she knew all that over-the-top physical stuff of earlier had been a temporary aberration she felt confident enough to risk a glance through her lashes at the personal devil she had exorcised and discovered his piercing eyes were fixed unblinkingly on her own face.

The intensity of his brooding contemplation released a flood of scalding heat that travelled through her body with appalling speed. The sexual inertia that accompanied the heat pinned her feet to the ground; though the feelings were centred low in her abdomen her entire body felt heavy and lethargic.

'You've taken your hair down,' he observed, examining with frank curiosity the wavy strands of moon-pale hair that fell to shoulder-blade level at the back and were cut shorter at the front and sides to frame her face with feathery strands. After a moment of contemplating the soft, face-framing style he gave his verdict. 'I like it.'

'You have no idea how completely indifferent I am to your approval,' she announced loudly.

The amused and extremely attractive grin that split

Finn's dark features only increased her antagonism and confusion.

'Are you going to walk down the street like that?' he asked, examining her bare feet.

'Would *you* like to walk around in these?' she asked him, waving the shoes in front of his nose. 'What are you looking at me like that for?' she added, suspicious of the abrupt shift of his expression.

His eyes moved to the shoes, which she was swinging pendulum-like on her finger, to her toes, covered only in colourless fine denier.

'I was just thinking that you look pretty different from the Hitchcock blonde who opened the door.'

Despite herself his comment intrigued her. 'Hitchcock as in...?'

'Cool blonde in the Grace Kelly mould. A class act.'

'What can I say? I was cheated; the make-up was meant to last twenty-four hours.'

'Have I said something to upset you?'

'Other than say I look a total mess...?'

'Don't be so over-sensitive.'

Easy for someone with an ego the size of Saint Paul's Cathedral to say. 'You said I *wasn't* a class act.'

'Is your sister as touchy as you?'

The mention of Annie reminded her of something she was continually in danger of forgetting—he wasn't here for the pleasure of her company or even to aggravate her. Finn had followed her because he had an agenda.

'When are you going to get it into your thick skull that I'm not going to help you?' she demanded. 'Or did you come to gloat?' she added as a bitter afterthought.

Yes that would be right, she thought, sliding him an unfriendly sideways look; he would be the petty, vindictive type to rub salt in the wound.

'So you didn't get it.'

Lucy gave a tight smile and was dismayed to feel her eyes fill with weak tears of self-pity. God knows what I'm going to do now, she wondered.

'They said I was overqualified.' She gave a self-deprecating shrug. 'I wasn't expecting to get it,' she admitted. 'I seriously doubt I'd even have had an interview if Annie hadn't put a word in for me—she runs the recruitment agency the company uses...I've no experience and none of the qualifications they asked for.'

A spasm of irritation disturbed the immobility of his dark features as he listened to her brutal self-assessment.

'Did you say anything along those lines in the interview?'

'Do you think I'm stupid or something?'

Something very something.

'Of course I didn't,' she snapped crossly when he didn't respond. 'Well, not in that way anyhow,' she added defensively as she recalled some of her responses.

He seized on her admission with a sigh. 'I thought as much. I could give you a few tips on interview technique if you like.'

'Thanks,' she said, flashing him a deeply insincere smile before taking longer than need be to smooth down her skirt—she was experiencing an extreme and growing reluctance to look directly at him. 'But Annie knows pretty much everything there is to know about such things and she's given me lots of good advice...I don't expect yours would be much different.' Or easier for me to follow, she thought dully.

'Do my homework, be confident—oh, and most importantly of all, don't under any circumstances be myself!'

As she heard her voice rise to a resentful shout, and then diminish to a shaky quaver, Lucy realised that she had minded a lot more than she'd let on even to herself the underlying message in Annie's well-meaning advice—nobody in their right mind would give the real Lucy a job!

She was standing there feeling totally mortified by this unplanned emotional outburst when Finn placed a hand lightly on the small of her back and drew her to one side as a large group of tourists with a harassed-looking guide at their head went by.

Very conscious of the fingers splayed across the base of her spine, Lucy heard him say quietly, 'Homework and confidence I agree with, but as for the matter of being yourself, your sister and I part company. I think you should always be yourself...' His hand dropped away.

Lucy's gaze switched from her cautious contemplation of her bare toes to his face. 'Why?'

His blue eyes scanned her face. 'Because you're not very good at pretending to be someone you're not, are you?'

This verdict stunned Lucy into silence.

'Of course, I'm not saying that being yourself will get you the job.'

'And why not?'

'Saying the first thing that comes into your head is not an attribute I'd personally look for in a personal assistant if I was the boss of a top advertising firm.'

'Now, that doesn't surprise me, on the other hand, I expect you put the ability to treat your every utterance as gospel top of the list...I suspect,' she continued in a shaky voice, 'that would be essential. You know, I'm incredibly impressed that you think you know me so well...after what?' She lifted her wrist. 'I've got a bus to catch.'

'Not so fast.' Finn caught her wrist.

For several seconds they remained there, eyes locked, neither prepared to give way. Lucy found her sense of urgency and purpose curiously slipping away.

'Don't go—come and have a coffee with me.'

A look of astonishment washed over Lucy's upturned face. 'Now, why would I do that?'

'Because I'm very entertaining company...? And,' he added, his determination undimmed by Lucy's derisive snort, 'you need cheering up. I am sorry about the job.'

'Don't be a hypocrite—you're not the least bit sorry!' Her hair whipped across her face to be impatiently pushed away as her mouth set in a mutinous line.

'Who's the hypocrite here?'

Despite the fact her conscience was clear his steady regard made her feel uncomfortable. 'What do you mean by that?' She scowled to hear the defensive note creep into her voice.

'I mean you didn't want the job to begin with.'

Lucy opened her mouth to deny this ridiculous claim and closed it again...could she see herself arriving at the office the same time every day, at the beck and call of some suit...?

'And you'd know, I suppose, being such an expert on what makes me tick.'

He didn't yet, but Finn was coming to the conclusion it might be interesting finding out...

'Well, you managed to come up with all the reasons in the book why you *shouldn't* have it.'

'This may be hard for someone who hasn't known a moment's self-doubt in his life to understand, but most people talk themselves down rather than beat their chest and announce to the world they're the best thing since sliced bread. That way if you lose you've already covered all the bases and if you win you can act pleasantly surprised.'

'I think you'll find the people that get the jobs are ready to announce to the world they're the best thing since sliced bread—it's called psyching out the opposition, Lucy. Be honest, did you really want the job…?'

'It was a very good job,' she deflected. Maybe his extraordinary eyes didn't just give the impression of being able to see your thoughts, maybe they actually could!

This fresh proof of her apparent inability to lie brought a wry smile to Finn's lips. 'There are other jobs, Lucy.'

She looked at him incredulously—was he trying to be sarcastic or did he really believe it was that easy? Well, maybe it was—for him.

'There are other jobs for people with experience and qualifications,' she threw angrily over her shoulder as she turned and began to walk away.

It could have looked comical, but it didn't. Finn decided it was because she carried the whole barefooted thing off with such natural dignity that the only glances she got were ones of admiration.

If ever a back had shouted 'angry' this slender one did. Finn watched her barefooted progress for a few moments longer taking male pleasure from the gentle, feminine sway of her hips before catching up with her. He recognised that there was a danger of his forgetting the reason he was here—to save his brother from himself and Annie Foster.

And who's going to save you, Finn? He didn't need the subconscious poke in the ribs; women like Lucy weren't part of his blueprint for life—he dated women who, like himself, were interested in a good time with no messy emotional complications. The moment they wanted to bond with his son or started stopping outside jewellery stores with prominent ring displays they were history.

Lucy Foster had to be the world's epicentre of emotional complications! Getting involved with her would be about as sensible as pitching your tent on the top of a volcano!

But what harm could a coffee do? And she might come

across with the information he needed…*sure, and hell froze over yesterday.*

Lucy had intended to ignore him but it wasn't easy to ignore someone who was equally indifferent to both icy dislike and hostile glares. She hoped against hope her breathless condition was caused by her efforts to outpace him and nothing more sinister. Deep down she knew that she was attracted to him in a way that frightened her, in a way that had nothing whatever to do with not liking him and everything to do with being unable to look at him without wondering what it would be like…

Oh, my, Luce, are you in trouble!

'If you don't come with me, what are you going to do?'

Lucy gave up the losing battle of trying to pretend he wasn't there.

'I'm going back to the flat, where I'm going to open a bottle of wine, eat copious amounts of Belgian chocolate until I feel sick and cry over a weepie video.'

'Well, you can do all of those things after you've had a coffee with me.'

If she hadn't known the real reason Finn was pursuing her she would have found this desire for her company quite flattering. She glanced at the tall, sensationally good-looking figure at her side and thought, No, actually, I wouldn't, I'd be wondering what the catch was.

Does that make me a realist or a cynic with low self-esteem…?

Well, whatever else she was it wasn't a coward.

She came to an abrupt dead stop. 'I can't tell you where they are because I just don't know.'

'Actually that wasn't why I asked you,' he replied and found he meant it.

Lucy searched his face and lowered her eyes quickly, afraid he would see the excitement that made her stomach muscles tighten and her knees wobble. She knew it was illogical, but she believed him.

'But first things first.'

'Where are we going?' This is not a date, Lucy, so stop acting as though it is. Following her own advice, she adopted a slightly bored expression.

Finn didn't seem to notice this as he patted the side of his nose and continued to behave in an irritatingly enigmatic fashion.

When he finally came to halt only a few yards down the road it was in front of a row of small, expensive-looking shops. Lucy looked at him expectantly.

'We need to go in here,' he said, taking her by the shoulders and propelling her firmly through the nearest doorway. 'You need shoes.'

And he helped her pick them, offering very unhelpful advice that both exasperated Lucy and made her laugh. In the end she chose a pair of cross trainers that probably looked absurd with Annie's slick designer suit, but sexy wasn't the look she was aiming for, something which she felt obliged to explain for Finn's benefit.

The amusement shimmering in his eyes abruptly blanked. 'It doesn't really matter—you'd look sexy in a bin-liner,' he observed in a detached manner that was totally at odds with the raw expression she glimpsed momentarily in his eyes.

CHAPTER FIVE

THE 'coffee shop' Finn took her to turned out to be a well-known restaurant, popular with the rich and famous which had been reopened after a greatly hyped and expensive refurbishment the previous week.

'I'm not sure this is a good idea,' she murmured uncomfortably after the waiter had taken their order for afternoon tea.

'You prefer coffee?'

'I wasn't talking about tea, I was talking about *this*,' she cried, lifting her eyes to the seriously gorgeous man sitting opposite her. It made no sense, she wasn't a masochist—she'd never waxed her legs in her life! So why was she here with a man who caused her entire body to ache with lust?

'Yeah, sorry about that; the last time I came here the theme was Edwardian...'

His censorious grimace as he surveyed the imitation steel girders that supported an equally imitation warehouse-style roof brought a reluctant smile to her lips.

'It's meant to be cutting edge.'

Finn leant forward across the table, his chin resting on his hands. 'You hate it,' he teased softly. 'Admit it.'

'All right, I hate it,' she admitted huskily.

'I knew it.' Leaning back in his chair, he fixed his narrowed gaze on an enormous mass of twisted metal that took pride of place on a raised dais in the centre of the room. 'And what do you suppose *that* is about?'

'I wasn't talking about the décor, Finn, I meant it isn't a good idea me being here with you.'

His eyes swept over her troubled face. 'I know you did,' he said softly. 'I was putting you at your ease.'

'That would be beyond even your capabilities,' she responded drily.

'Why?'

'Well, you...' Her eyelashes fluttered downwards. 'You make me...I don't feel comfortable around you.' She saw the speculative narrowing of his eyes and hurried on. 'Because I have to watch what I say in case you trick me into telling you something about my sister.' Well, it was *part* of the truth.

Finn's jaw clenched as he dragged a hand over his sleek hair. 'Can't we leave them out of this for a moment?'

Lucy couldn't believe what she was hearing; neither, though she didn't know it, could Finn.

'You're the one with the overwhelming need to live your brother's life for him,' she pointed out tartly. 'Hasn't it occurred to you he'll never learn how to fix the things he breaks if you do it for him? You're not fighting your kid brother's battles in the playground any more, Finn.'

'I never did.' He intercepted her quizzical look and with obvious reluctance elaborated. 'Our parents split up when we were quite small. Con stayed with Dad in Ireland and Mom went back to the States and took me. We only saw one another for the holidays—summer in the holiday house in West Cork and Christmas in New York.'

'Oh, that's sad,' she responded with spontaneous sympathy.

When their own father had died it had been to each other she and Annie had turned. She didn't like to think about what it would have been like without that mutual support. She knew a couple who had let the children decide for themselves who they lived with, effectively forcing them to reject one parent. At the time she could remember thinking what an awful burden to place on a child's shoulders. Had that happened to Finn?

Lucy sometimes wondered why children who had experienced first-hand what happened when a marriage went bad ever got married themselves; divorce was tough on kids, but then fortunately kids were incredibly resilient creatures.

'Is your mother American, then?' she asked, trying to disguise the empathy that brought a thickness to her throat behind a matter-of-fact manner.

For a moment she thought he wasn't going to reply.

'They both are—native New Yorkers.' He paused while the waiter delivered their tea and scones. 'Milk?' Lucy nodded. 'Con and I were both born there,' he continued as he expertly poured the tea. 'Dad's from Irish stock and Mom's Italian-American; he went home one summer to find his roots and decided to stay there.'

'Italian!' she exclaimed. 'Oh, that explains…' Embarrassed, she cut off the rest of her observation and lowered her gaze.

'Explains what?'

'Your colouring…' *Colouring* seemed too insipid a term to cover the vital glow of toasted gold skin. A distracted expression slid into her eyes as they moved over the well-developed, lean contours of his sinewed, hair-roughened forearms. 'You're very…' *Beautiful…?*

She raised the cup to her lips and under cover of taking a sip slid a covetous look at him from beneath her lashes. What she saw was the average female fantasy brought to life and, unlike a fantasy, he was real and therefore far more dangerous.

Beautiful…? Absolutely.

'Dark,' she finished thickly. 'Didn't your mother like Ireland?' she added, anxious to shift the conversation away from matters pertaining to his physical appearance.

'She liked it fine for a vacation, but she's a big-city girl and she missed her work.'

'What does she do?'

'She's a journalist, they both were, only Dad swopped his job as the economics editor of a national daily to run a local weekly.'

'But now you live in Ireland?'

'Not exclusively. We are based in Dublin but we have strong links with the States...and you, Lucy, I suppose you're a product of the perfect nuclear family?' Did such a thing exist these days outside popular fiction?

'I don't know about perfect, but I had a happy childhood, yes.'

'And you're still close with your parents?'

'Dad died when I was thirteen,' she explained quietly. 'It was hard for Mum, she sacrificed a lot for Annie and me, but she met a lovely man and they got married a couple of months ago, which I'm sure is of absolutely no interest to you...'

'What makes you say that?'

He was far too clever to come out with a direct contradiction. 'Do you expect me to believe that your main priority isn't still stopping your brother and my sister getting married?' she flung accusingly.

'No, I don't expect you to believe that, but neither am I trying to lull you into a false sense of security before I use my fiendish mind probe to extract the information I require.'

'This isn't a joke.'

'How many hotels do you think they have in the Lake District?'

This totally unrelated question brought a frown of irritation to her brow. 'How on earth should I know?' she snapped.

'Do you think more than a hundred would be a safe bet...?'

'The Lake District is one of the most popular tourist destinations in the country; what do you think?'

'I think my secretary is going to be extremely ticked off with me.' He responded to Lucy's confused look with a wry grin. 'At the moment,' he explained, 'Elspeth is ringing her way through the *Yellow Pages*. Of course, Con's tastes don't run to simple B&Bs, so that limits the search—he's a five-star-luxury man.'

Lucy's jaw dropped. 'You did that when you left the flat?' she ejaculated incredulously.

'Always have a secondary plan of action, Lucy,' he advised solemnly.

Plan of action? The idea that any rational thought processes had brought her here was one she was too honest to subscribe to...she'd been responding to nothing more rational than a totally *irrational* desire to prolong her contact with this man. What she was feeling might be superficial and shallow but that didn't mean it wasn't strong.

'No, what was your secondary plan?'

'Mine?' she echoed blankly.

'What did you plan to do if you didn't get the job?'

Lucy shrugged and pushed a scone around her plate. 'I don't really make plans. I just go with the flow...let life surprise me.' A born worrier, she had not the faintest idea why she'd said something that made her sound, depending on your viewpoint, either incredibly laid-back or feckless.

'And does it?'

Well, it certainly had today.

Her eyes flickered to his face and fell quickly away as

if she was afraid to look at him. Maybe she was? Which begged the question, why? He felt his body react strongly to the possibilities.

'Yes, but they're not always nice surprises.'

Finn maintained a politely attentive expression while wondering if she would consider the suggestion they forget the tea and go straight to bed a *nice* one? There was nothing very unusual about a bit of harmless speculation concerning a woman you were attracted to. It was the overwhelming urge he had to follow through that sobered him up fast.

'What about your book?' Finn cleared his throat and made some unnecessary adjustments to his cuffs.

Lucy looked up. 'My book?'

'This might be a good time to do something about that. Move past the first chapter, or are you blocked?'

'The writing is just something I do for me…I'm not actually a *writer*.'

'Are you always so negative? You don't expect to get the job; you don't expect to get published?' His raised voice caused the people sitting on the next table to look across. Finn gave them back a black look that made them look away quickly.

She reacted angrily to this accusation. 'I'm an extremely positive person. I'm not negative, I'm realistic,' she elaborated.

'Why don't you stop moaning about what you're not and make use of what you are? You must have experience at something…a woman doesn't get to be what…' his narrowed eyes travelled over her face and figure assessingly '…twenty-three, -four…?'

Lucy pressed a hand to her throat, where a pulse was pounding visibly. 'Twenty-six,' she replied huskily.

There had been nothing remotely sexual in his objective

study, but her body had reacted shockingly to the brush of his eyes.

She had travelled Europe, encountered and had no problem coping when she came to the attention of sexy Spaniards, amorous Italians and romantically inclined Greeks—but none had had this effect upon her. She had been able to look at their mouths without wondering what it would feel like to have their lips come crashing down upon hers. She had not experienced urges to sink her fingers deep into their hair…hair which in many cases had been as dark and lush as Finn Fitzgerald's.

What was so different about him?

She was obviously suffering from some sort of serious hormonal imbalance.

There was probably a perfectly good herbal remedy for this sort of thing.

'Twenty-six is no spring chicken.'

'Thank you for that—unemployable, *and* past my sell-by date…all I need now is to walk under a bus and my day is complete.'

His lips twitched but he didn't respond to her acid humour. 'Unless you've hardly been existing inside a vacuum for the last few years, you must have been doing something.'

Her chin lifted as she tried to ignore the humiliating way her sensitised nipples were chafing against her bra. 'My last job was as a waitress.'

'And were you a good waitress?' he asked with what appeared genuine interest.

Lucy's feathery brows drew into a puzzled line at his response. She knew for a fact that Annie had avoided telling her upwardly mobile friends that her sister was working as a waitress, so she had taken Finn Fitzgerald's snooty reaction for granted…his interested attitude seemed not only genuine but also totally lacking any snobbishness.

Lucy felt irrationally annoyed with him for his lack of prejudice.

'I was a very good waitress,' she announced with some pride.

It was true, she had enjoyed immensely her stint working in a small family restaurant set in the winding streets of the charming Plaka region at the foot of the Acropolis. She had even ended up teaching the recently widowed owner to keep the accounts which had previously been his late wife's province.

'So you've experience in catering…' he noted. 'What did you do before that?'

Lucy turned her exasperated gaze on him. 'What are you, a frustrated careers advisor? Why are you doing this?' she demanded bluntly.

She didn't for a moment think Finn Fitzgerald, who was part of an operation that had a multimillion-pound turnover, could actually be *interested* in her modest career prospects.

'What,' she added suspiciously, 'are you after?'

His cynical mouth lifted at the corners. 'I like that about you—you always think the best of a man.'

His tone made Lucy flush. 'Thinking the best of a man can cause a girl a lot of heartache.' The flicker of speculation in his eyes made her wish she'd kept this opinion to herself.

'Have you considered the possibility that I might feel some degree of responsibility for you not getting the job?'

'You?' she ejaculated.

'I'll take that as a no, shall I?' he said drily.

'Why should you feel responsible?'

'And I did make you late.'

In her experience a man with *any* sense of responsibility was something of a rarity.

'Oh, that!' Lucy shrugged. 'It wouldn't have made any difference; I wouldn't have got it even if I had got there dead on time, and before you start,' she said, forestalling any further unflattering readings of her character, 'that statement has nothing whatever to do with lack of self-belief or lack of ambition. I just didn't want the job…you were right.'

'What did you do before the waitressing job, Lucy?'

Lucy gave a gasp of exasperation; the man didn't know when to quit and this interrogation had gone on long enough. 'I was a nanny. Now, if you don't mind…' It was obviously time to be blunt.

'A nanny.' He looked thoughtful. 'Now, that *is* interesting.'

Lucy was puzzled by his apparent interest. 'I don't see why and actually officially I was an au pair, but I spent most of my time with the children.'

Finn saw her struggle and fail to prevent her rigid expression softening as she mentioned the children. 'You enjoyed that? You like children?'

'For heaven's sake, I…*Good God*!' she gasped, her horror-struck eyes riveted on a couple who had just emerged from a door at the far end of the room. She hunched her shoulders so that she was hidden behind Finn's broader frame. 'Don't move!' she hissed urgently.

'I wasn't going to,' he revealed. 'But I thought you were. I'm glad you decided to stay, but,' he added as she appeared to be trying to shrink, 'what are you doing?'

This was the girl in the snapshot, not so carefree-looking, but the same girl. The one he had wanted to kiss.

Actually he still did.

Reacting to an instinct that said 'hide,' Lucy grabbed his hand and slid into the chair beside him.

'This isn't a joke.'

'I can see that.'

'I've just seen someone I don't particularly want to... No, don't look...!' Curling her fingers over the hard angle of his jaw, she urgently turned his head back towards her.

The action caused their eyes to connect; what she saw in his made Lucy catch her breath, and the pupils of her wide eyes expanded rapidly until only a thin ring of amber iris remained.

After several moments of immobility she shook her head like someone waking up from a dream and with a startled gasp would have withdrew her hand if his own hadn't come up to cover it.

'Please?'

For a moment Finn didn't respond to the husky plea but then with a shrug and a wry look in his eyes he released her fingers. Lucy experienced a somewhat ambivalent re-action to his co-operation as if part of her hadn't wanted to be released.

Lucy forgot her own strictures and poked her head around his shoulder. With a gasp she withdrew it and she closed her eyes. 'They're coming this way...they'll see me unless...if we get up and I walk that side of you we might make it to the door...on three; one, two...'

'I hate to be a wet blanket...' Finn murmured as she welded herself to his side. 'Heck, I always wanted to be a spy, but they're going to think we're skipping out without paying the bill and one brush with the law a day is enough for me.'

'It's too late—he's seen me! He's coming over!' she said in a dull voice of dread. 'And *she's* with him! How do I look?' she demanded, raising her eyes to Finn's face.

Just when she needed him to say something the man who had far too much to say for himself as a rule seemed to have lost his ability to speak. He was looking at her with a peculiarly blank expression on his spectacularly handsome face.

'You look fine,' he judged finally.

Fine. Her hands clenched into white-knuckled fists at her sides. Well, what did you expect him to tell you, Lucy... that you're a raving beauty maybe...?

'After today,' she announced despondently, 'I just can't take this. For God's sake,' she added as Rupert got close enough for her to see the whites of his eyes, 'don't just stand there like a shop dummy, *do something*!'

When she made this totally unreasonable demand it didn't actually occur to her that Finn would respond and even if she had she would never, not in million years, have imagined that he would do so in the manner he did!

Like someone deep under water fighting her way to the surface, Lucy gasped for air. Initially the face of the man bending over her was a dark blur but as the blood pounding in her temples slowed to a dull throb his features slowly slipped into focus.

Eyes wide and shocked, her body still racked by intermittent fine tremors, her thoughts showing a disastrous tendency to drift off into warm, dreamy directions, Lucy lifted a shaky hand to her lips; they felt bruised and tender.

CHAPTER SIX

'You kissed me.'

The surface of her hot skin prickled as Lucy relived the moment when his tongue had parted her lips. Her stomach muscles quivered and an unfocused glaze slid into her eyes as she trailed her fingers across her mouth.

She shook her head to clear the fog in her brain.

'You kissed me!' she repeated, indignation belatedly entering her voice.

'You asked me to do something,' he reminded her innocently.

You're acting as if you've never been kissed before, Lucy. It was a sad reflection of her sex life that she hadn't, not like that anyhow! She felt weird, she felt excited, she felt a dozen things that were so outside her experience she couldn't even put a name to them.

This would never do. It occurred to her that in the interests of damage limitation she ought to be treating the incident with the same sort of casualness he was.

Calling upon her deepest reserves of discipline, she took a deep calming breath.

'Do *something*, not *that*,' she hissed in a driven undertone.

He looked into her tawny eyes and gave a wolfish smile. 'What can I say?' He shrugged. 'I used my initiative.'

'The same initiative that has put your hand on my bottom?' The other was resting on the back of her head and his fingertips were massaging her scalp. The effect was kind of hypnotic.

'That's the lumbar region of your back. Now, *this* is your bottom,' he explained as his hand slipped southwards and settled comfortably over the feminine curve of her bottom. And a very nice bottom it was too.

'When I need a lesson in anatomy off you I'll ask for it…' she cried, pulling away but not before he'd felt the heat of her skin.

She felt the rumble of laughter in his chest and her humiliation increased tenfold. 'Now, there's a thought to cheer my lonely nights,' he murmured.

'You…you…' Lucy spluttered, wrenching herself free of his arms. She stood there glaring at him, her arms crossed protectively over her heaving chest as she tried to catch her breath.

'This is nice, isn't it? We're bonding.'

Lucy was about to tell him that he was insane, when it hit her—they might not be *bonding*, as he put it, but fighting with and being kissed by Finn—especially being kissed—was actually more excitement than she had had for a long time. This might merely be a sad reflection on her social life or it might be a symptom of something more serious. She wasn't *enjoying* it exactly, but she did feel more alive…it was all deeply disturbing.

'Lucy, it is you, isn't it?' The hearty cry that cut through her ruminations was almost welcome.

Before turning Lucy shot Finn, who had been observing the expressions flitting across her face with interest, a fulminating look as she tore her eyes from his. Taking a deep breath, she pinned a brilliant, vacuous smile on her face and turned around.

'Rupert, what a surprise…' Her smile grew even more wooden as her eyes slid to the woman standing beside him—a petite brunette with big brown eyes and a delicate look. Lucy knew the delicacy was highly deceptive, but it worked a treat with men in whom she brought out the protective hunter-gatherer instincts.

'And Helen too...how...' Lucy broke off, unable to bring herself to express pleasure. 'It's been a long time,' she substituted awkwardly.

The woman whom Rupert had married instead of her smiled back with equal insincerity.

'You look well, Rupert,' Lucy observed with composure. 'Marriage must be suiting you.' It seemed strange looking at him and realising that if things had gone differently it might have been her standing there.

Why had the words 'lucky' and 'escape' suddenly sprung to mind?

'I hardly recognised you, Lucy.' Rupert flicked open the button on his double-breasted suit, revealing the weight gain she'd immediately noticed was not restricted to his face. 'You look well...*marvellous*!'

Lucy marvelled at the perversity of men; ironically Rupert was looking at her with far more admiration than he had when they were supposedly engaged, but more surprising than this was the fact his admiration meant nothing whatever to her.

'Doesn't she just?' Finn murmured above her.

His rich, warm voice, combined with the hand he slid possessively around her waist, was a statement of ownership, a man saying, she's mine, hands off.

Lucy's head lifted, their eyes met and stomach muscles fluttered. Finn's eyes contained the visual version of what she had heard in his voice.

This man was one hell of an actor, she decided shakily. Now wasn't the moment to consider the alternative—that he might not be acting.

Lucy was actually quite glad that Finn wasn't a man happy to stay in the background, though she doubted he often found himself in that position and certainly not on this occasion—Rupert and Helen had both been casting speculative looks in his direction.

Whatever the motivation for his contribution it took the attention from her, which could only be a good thing, and there was nothing much under the circumstances she could do about the hand around her waist—*did she actually want to…?*

She dragged her attention away from Finn and discovered Rupert and his wife were waiting expectantly for her to introduce Finn. Well, she could hardly deny she knew him after they'd seen him kiss her, especially as she'd kissed him back. Enthusiastically.

Oh, God!

Lucy experienced a surge of wildly conflicting emotions as she recalled the sensual stab of his tongue into her mouth and the searing possession of his lips.

Maybe this is post-traumatic shock, the trauma in the instance being a kiss, she mused with a faintly desperate attempt at whimsical humour.

'This is Finn Fitzgerald.' She turned her head slightly and fixed her glassy gaze on Finn's ear. 'Finn, this is Dr Rupert Drake and his wife, Helen,' she explained, turning back to Rupert and the petite figure beside him.

'Fitzgerald?' Helen entered the conversation for the first time. 'Didn't I see you on that television programme the other week about the revival in the Irish economy?'

'The thing they did on the faces behind Celtic Tiger economy? No, that would have been my brother. Connor is more photogenic than me. I'm strictly the back-room boy.'

Helen, who obviously wasn't sure how to respond to Finn's sardonic humour, smiled uncertainly. 'Yes, his accent, it seemed more…'

'I've spent more time in the States,' Finn inserted smoothly.

'I always think that success is nine parts luck and one part talent.'

'Rupert, really, what a thing to say!' his wife responded looking embarrassed by the truculent observation.

She needn't have bothered on Finn's account, Lucy thought, glancing at his strong, imperturbable profile; the slight was like water off the proverbial duck's back with him. She knew she was looking at a man who knew that he was good at what he did, and didn't need other people to validate what he did.

'I wasn't suggesting that you're not most able...' Rupert added grudgingly.

'Able!' Helen shot an apologetic look in Finn's direction. 'His brother said that he's considered a genius by everyone in the industry!'

Lucy, who had a very clear recollection of implying he hung on to the coat tails of his brother's success, felt like groaning.

'No, your husband's right.' In contrast to the other man, Finn looked totally relaxed. 'Being in the right place at the right time helps and rumours of my genius have been greatly exaggerated.' There was challenge in his eyes as he captured Lucy's gaze. 'I'm just wildly talented,' he informed them blandly with a grin.

Rupert, whose admiring glance strayed constantly to Lucy, much to his wife's obvious annoyance, spoke up once more.

'We were here for lunch with the owners. They wanted to express their gratitude. Helen is responsible for this,' Rupert explained with a proud flourish in the direction of the large metallic modern sculpture.

Lucy made the appropriate admiring noises while think-

ing this explained the slight slur in Rupert's speech, and
his lack of inhibitions when it came to ogling her legs. The
owners must have been very hospitable hosts and Rupert
never had been able to refuse a freebie, or hold his drink.

'So, what are you doing with yourself these days, Lucy?'

'Actually I've had an interview.' Lucy heard the truth
spring automatically from her lips with a sense of exasperation—a lie would have avoided the inevitable enquiries
about her success.

But even when her brain wasn't working now, she was
too distracted by the fact Finn's long fingers had splayed
over the crest of her right hip, and the deceptively casual
gesture had her superglued against his side so closely she
could feel every inch of his iron-hard thigh. Images in her
head of tanned brown skin covered in a dusting of dark hair
and strong muscles flexing appeared in her head and refused to be banished.

The images combined with the things the apparently un-
conscious—*she didn't think!*—stroking sensations of his
long fingers were doing to her nervous system, made it hard
for her to think let alone invent plausible lies.

On the other hand she was pretty sure that Finn
Fitzgerald, who had no inhibitions she could detect concerning lying, could have woven a world-class web of de-
ceit in the epicentre of a hurricane.

Talking of high-pressure zones, there was one building
inside her that made the blood thrumming through her ears
pound.

One fingertip dipped a little lower, skimming over the
sensitive hollow of her thigh. Lucy audibly sucked in her
breath as the intimate ache between her thighs made her
swallow hard. The arm about her waist automatically tightened as her knees sagged.

Lucy smiled at the looks of enquiry. 'A touch of...' she

felt the silent laughter vibrate in Finn's chest and almost lost it '…migraine.' She didn't have to feign the pain when she lifted a hand artistically to her temple.

She had reached the point where she didn't care if they believed her lame excuse or not; she just wanted to get out of here so that she could tell Finn exactly what she thought of him.

The thought of what she would say to him was the only thing keeping her going!

'How horrid; I hope it didn't affect your interview, Lucy, and I hope you didn't go wearing those.' Helen laughed, her eyes on Lucy's feet.

'Do you like them? I helped her choose them.'

'Help! Is that what you call it?'

Rupert's expression grew increasingly sour as he listened to this interchange. 'You always were an original, Luce,' he recalled wistfully.

Nobody would have guessed from his attitude that her *originality* had been one of the many things Rupert had listed to support his claim they were totally incompatible. Only back then he'd called it her erratic behaviour.

Fragmented images of the past crowded into Lucy's head.

'The university community is a very conservative community, Lucy, hierarchical; you can't go chatting to the vice-chancellor as if he's one of the boys.'

'Don't worry, I didn't tell him any rude jokes,' Lucy, puzzled by his concern, had joked back.

Now, of course, she knew he'd been afraid something she had inadvertently let slip would make the college authorities aware of how much input she had had in the research Rupert had presented as his own work.

'And it's not even as if we're *really* engaged.'

Lucy looked at her bare finger—when he'd said they

didn't need a ring to confirm their commitment she'd thought it was very romantic. 'Don't you think you might have said this a bit sooner…like a year or so? Or even before you started sleeping with whatsername?'

'Helen; she's an art student.'

'Did they give their decision or are you waiting for that phone call? I always hate that…'

Helen's crisp, upper-crust diction brought Lucy back to the present with a resounding thud.

She responded to the smooth insincerity of the other woman with a repressed sigh…time to ruin the illusion and go back to being Lucy without the high-powered job and exciting prospects. 'Actually I—'

'Actually I was about to make Lucy a better offer when you arrived.' Finn's smooth interruption contained just enough teasing ambiguity to leave the listener unsure whether this offer he spoke of was of a personal or business nature.

'You were?' Lucy heard herself say stupidly.

She met his amused eyes and bit her lip, a vivid blush spreading rapidly over her face…of course he wasn't, you, idiot.

When Finn placed a finger under her chin and tilted her head up, though, she would have preferred to look any-where, but short of creating a scene Lucy had no option but to look into his shimmering blue eyes. She had steeled herself for his mockery but not the rampant hunger in his eyes. It blasted through her feeble defence mechanisms, leaving her wide open and helpless.

Eyes still locked to hers, he ran his thumb over her full lower lip. Her sensitive stomach muscles responded in-stantly to the contact by quivering violently. For one horrid moment she thought her knees were literally going to fold under her.

This might be amusing for him but she didn't feel much like laughing, in fact her body's weak response to his raw sexuality filled her with deep shame not untouched by despair.

Surely I'm more than a bunch of chemical reactions and hormones!

'Oh, how exciting.'

Lucy was momentarily diverted from the contemplation of her own weakness by the sound in the younger woman's voice of the sort of envy that she had once dreamt vengefully of putting there. Never in those far-off dreams of retribution had she imagined it occurring quite this way!

'I'm hoping the wine over dinner will soften her up.' His thumb traced the line of her jaw. 'All's fair in love and business, hey, sweetheart?'

Unable to withstand any more of this play-acting, Lucy tore her chin from his grip. She turned in time to see a distinctly petulant expression spread across Rupert's face as he watched them.

'I thought it was war.'

Finn, who so far had paid the other man scant attention, suddenly turned his penetrating gaze on her ex. Having been the focus of his soul-stripping scrutiny, Lucy wasn't surprised that Rupert seemed to find the experience uncomfortable though she seriously doubted his discomfort had much in common with her own!

'Much the same thing,' Finn replied finally with a look on his hard-edged face which Lucy suspected his business rivals would have recognised and respected.

She had never doubted that Finn was capable of acts of cold, clinical ruthlessness to get his own way, but seeing it illustrated so clearly sent a chill shivering down Lucy's spine.

In contrast to his hostile manner with Rupert, when he

turned to Helen he was all charm. 'So…Helen, you're an artist?'

'No, Helen is an art consultant,' Rupert declared proudly. 'She commissioned the William Napier,' he said with a grand gesture towards the large, centrally situated metallic structure.

Lucy tilted her head to one side but she still couldn't figure out what this mass of twisted metal was meant to represent. 'Very impressive,' she said, conscious that some response was expected.

'Yes, breathtaking, isn't it?' Rupert agreed. 'It's so organic…' he enthused.

'You took the words right out of my mouth,' Finn murmured.

Rupert, oblivious to the sardonic undertones that made Lucy cringe, nodded happily.

'Yes, everyone was knocked out. Everyone who is anyone was here at the unveiling, you know.' He went on to list the names of these exalted personages, most of whom Lucy had never heard of.

'Art consultant…does that mean you tell people with no taste what they should buy…?'

Helen sent a condescending smile in Finn's direction. Even without looking to see what his reaction was, Lucy instinctively knew this was a mistake—Finn was not the sort of man to sit there meekly while someone patronised him. She almost felt sorry for the other woman—*almost*.

'It's not that simple,' she explained with a serious expression. 'Leaving aside the corporate work we do, there are an incredible number of people who have money to invest but not time to research the subject.'

'And would it be such a disaster if they bought something to put on their wall just because they liked the look of it?'

Helen's tinkling laughter rang out. 'You're joking…right?'

'No.'

Helen looked shocked by his blunt response. 'Think of all the money a person could lose on a bad investment.'

'Think of all the pleasure they could get by looking at something they liked.'

This was too anarchic a concept for Helen, who chose to think he was joking. *'Seriously,'* she said, 'if ever you need any advice I'd be quite happy—'

'Thanks for the offer,' Finn interrupted, a shade of impatience entering his voice. 'But actually I'm not a big fan of leasing out sections of my life to experts. In my own clumsy, inexpert way I'll carry on buying my own art, drinking my own wine and doing my own kissing, even though it's not a financially efficient use of my resources. I guess,' he drawled, 'I'm funny that way and actually,' he added with a wicked look in Lucy's direction, 'some people think I'm getting quite good at the DIY.'

After that nobody seemed inclined to prolong the conversation. Lucy was amused by the notable lack of enthusiasm in Rupert's limp *We must get together some time* as they made their goodbyes.

From the expression on his face he received Finn's message loud and clear. The irony was that after Finn's brilliant performance Rupert probably thought that the other man's antagonism was that of a man saying 'hands off' to any prospective rival.

Lucy didn't know which was funnier—the idea of Finn being seriously interested in her or that anyone who had Finn as a lover would even look at Rupert!

As her eyes were drawn to Finn's strong, aesthetically perfect profile she found herself speculating once more about what sort of lover he would make. It was a place that she knew it was best not to go but, like Pandora's box, once Lucy had started she couldn't put the lid back on.

Casual or demanding…? Loyal or did he have a wandering eye? Her own eyes had been doing some unplanned wandering, and as her speculation led her away from the general and towards more explicit details that might be involved in being Finn Fitzgerald's lover she dropped her eyes guiltily.

Some deluded women thought they could change a man once they got him, and they didn't mind making a few personal compromises to achieve that end. In Finn's case his faults were probably half of his attraction to the opposite sex. What would she change about Finn, she wondered, if she had the chance…?

Nothing.

It was at that moment that Lucy knew she needed to come up with a fast solution to her immediate problem—namely putting as much space between herself and Finn Fitzgerald as was humanly possible! After a feverish examination of her options she decided the best way to make Finn lose interest in following her was to ignore him.

Men with outsized egos like him didn't like to be ignored, they liked to be the centre of attention, so it seemed safe to assume that if he was starved of attention he wouldn't hang around for long.

On the other hand it would be just her luck if he decided to look on it as a challenge…?

CHAPTER SEVEN

THEY reached the pavement but Lucy never actually got to test either theory. It was hard bordering on impossible to ignore a man of Finn's physical dimensions when he placed himself directly in your path.

She swallowed as her eyes reluctantly made the journey from the mid-point of his broad chest to his face; meeting his eyes was like a blow low in her stomach.

'That,' she told him, her voice shaking, 'was an excruciatingly embarrassing situation made a hundred times worse by you! What did you think you were doing?'

'That's all the thanks I get.' The frown lines across his broad brow deepened and against his will the furious words exploded from him. 'What I can't figure out is what the hell you ever saw in the guy.'

Lucy stiffened with annoyance at the scornful censure in his tone. 'Are you talking about Rupert?'

Her chilly disdain bounced right off him. With a mumbled impatient imprecation he pulled her to one side a little way from the steady flow of pedestrians along the busy road, just avoiding collision with a man who wielded his umbrella like a spear.

'Lover boy,' he snarled with studied insolence.

'What have you got against Rupert?'

'You mean other than the fact the man is a total loser?'

Lucy arched a brow ironically and stepped away from him. 'Another of your lightning character assessments...?'

One which, incidentally, she was in full agreement with—not that she had any intention of telling him so. The more she considered his attitude the angrier she got—where did Finn Fitzgerald get off thinking he could pass comment, not to mention judgement, on her personal life to begin with?

'How would you like it if I started slagging off your friends?'

'Are you trying to tell me he's not a loser?'

'Rupert is considered extremely intelligent.' Especially by himself. 'He's a professor of ancient history.'

It was the idea that she couldn't see the guy for what he obviously was that made Finn unable to maintain his silence even when he knew he was only alienating her.

The same Finn who usually avoided the minefield of offering advice, well-meaning or otherwise, heard himself observe with stern disapproval, 'The wife looked pig sick too, which is hardly surprising.'

'Pity you didn't realise that earlier. I know she's a bit full of herself, but did you have to be so rude to her...?'

'I wasn't talking about me,' he retorted. 'I'm talking about the way her husband was drooling over you.' His lip curled expressively.

Lucy blushed. 'He was not drooling!'

'I felt damned sorry for the woman.'

'*You did?*' No doubt the reason he was looking at her as though she was a major disappointment would reveal itself in due course, but right now Lucy was completely bemused.

'Well, it was obviously a shock for her, seeing you there.' His eyes dropped, moving slowly down the slender length of her body. Lucy saw the muscles in his brown throat move as he swallowed. '*Looking like that.*'

Lucy's own gaze followed the direction of his eyes...so she might no longer be the immaculate fashion plate she had been earlier, but she didn't look bad enough to justify his apparent abhorrence.

'You mean it offends someone as fastidious as Helen that I wear trainers and appear in public without full make-up…?'

The lush screen of his long lashes lifted and a raw gasp was drawn from Lucy as their eyes collided. Mesmerised by the raw, glowing hunger in Finn's piercing blue eyes, she had absolutely no control over the furtive shiver of forbidden excitement that slipped down her spine.

He shook his head. 'That you appear in public looking the way *she* couldn't look if she spent the next year in a beauty salon,' he contradicted hardly.

Lucy raised a hand to her head—someone inside her skull was practising with a sledgehammer. 'Was…was that a compliment?' she mumbled in disbelief.

Finn's jaw clenched. 'What's wrong, Lucy, are you not content with one man making a total idiot of himself over you—you want me too?'

Her cheeks burned with mortification at the accusation. 'I…I don't want you,' she stuttered.

'That's not the message I've been getting.'

'Then you're…'

'I'm what, Lucy…?' he prompted. 'Deluded, full of myself? I don't think so. How long has it been over?' he added abruptly.

'How long has what been over?' Her distracted whisper was barely audible.

'The affair, Lucy,' he replied heavily.

Lucy blinked. *'What did you say…?'*

'Or is it still going on?'

'I really don't have the faintest—'

'Did the wife find out?' he persisted. 'I suppose they usually do.'

Suddenly she knew what he was saying and her confusion was converted in the blink of an eye to fury. 'How dare you…?' she quivered. 'You sanctimonious, hypocrit-ical…' she gritted through clenched teeth.

'For God's sake, don't try telling me you didn't sleep with the man—it was screamingly obvious from the way the little rat was looking at you,' Finn sneered.

'If I had slept with an entire football team it would be none of your business, but actually, yes, I did sleep with Rupert,' Lucy agreed with a hard little laugh that made Finn's nostrils flare with distaste.

'Oh, I know how you feel—I feel a bit sick when I think about it too.' Rupert had been her first love, and sometimes she had thought that he might be her last. 'But it's almost obligatory these days when you're engaged to someone to sleep with them, not that we actually waited that long,' she admitted. 'I thought I'd found *the one*, you see; I could hardly wait to lose my—'

The soft, sibilant sound of Finn's startled curse stemming the flow of her confidences brought home the inadvisability of spilling your guts to someone who very probably didn't want to hear all your deepest, darkest secrets.

'Then you were the…?'

She lifted her head and nodded; Finn looked pretty pale under his smooth, even tan. 'That's right, I was the one who got cheated on—a woman scorned!'

Her theatrical gesture distracted but did not hide the hurt in her eyes—at least not from Finn, who closed his own. *'Oh, hell!'*

'And what makes it even funnier was I really was the last to know. The entire department knew before me,' she revealed in a flat little voice.

'You worked at the university?'

'I was a post-grad student, Rupert's research assistant. He wasn't a professor then.' Marrying the vice-chancellor's daughter had turned out to be a very canny career move.

Lucy felt a surge of guilt at the catty thought—whatever else he was, Rupert was a good academic.

Finn's fists clenched at his sides. 'I knew, I just *knew* he was a total sleaze the moment I saw him!'

Only the constraints of modern society which got unreasonably sniffy about a man administering justice himself stopped Finn marching back into the building and spoiling the sleaze's dental work right there and then.

'I'm naturally elated to be able to confirm your instincts were right.'

Given the choice between being looked at like a scarlet woman or a pathetic object of pity, Lucy would have plumped for the former every time.

'I am not as bitter and twisted as I sound; it was a long time ago and I'm totally over it. I'm not telling you any of this because I think it's your business.' Then just why are you telling him, Luce? 'Still, this has been quite a revelation; I had no idea you were such a pious, sanctimonious—'

'All right, point taken,' he grunted. 'I jumped to conclusions…I'm sorry,' he grated harshly.

Lucy examined his brooding expression and the dark band of soft colour across the crests of his sharply etched cheekbones.

'Do you feel a total idiot now for getting it wrong? Please say you do,' she pleaded. 'It'll make me feel a lot better about making a fool of myself, babbling on like that,' she finished uncomfortably.

The silence between them stretched. 'I feel a total, absolute idiot,' he confirmed.

'Good, then let's call it quits.'

'You could have wrung a lot more humiliation out of this situation.' And most women he knew would have.

'I'd sooner forget it.'

But had she forgotten Rupert? 'Do you think that could be classed as our first argument?'

'I don't know.' It seemed to Lucy that their communication so far had consisted of one long argument, interspersed by some steamy moments when their bodies did some unscheduled communication. Just thinking about that communication sent her temperature soaring. 'But it will definitely be our last.'

'How can you be so sure?'

'I can be sure because I'm going that way.' She nodded over her shoulder. 'And you are not.'

'So this is goodbye.'

The way he said it made it sound awfully final—which it was and a very good thing too, she told herself briskly. 'Goodbye,' she agreed.

'Will you miss me?'

Miss fighting, being insulted and having her hormones in a constant state of chaos? Only a total fool would think that was a state to be desired.

'Not in the least,' she told him. Well, telling him about the empty feeling she got inside when she thought about never seeing him again was not actually a sound option for a girl who enjoyed her celibate existence.

'I thought you were starting to like me.'

'Was this before or after you called me a home-breaker?'

Finn winced. 'That was a mistake.'

'No, kissing me was a mistake, *that* was you being a self-righteous, hypocritical jerk.'

'Kissing you was not a mistake...'

But me mentioning it was, she thought, trying to maintain a tough front and failing in a big way. Their eyes met and a wave of paralysing lust washed over her.

'It was a great pleasure.' Finn watched the colour rush to her cheeks. 'At least I thought so and you seemed to enjoy it at the time too.' He watched his sly observation turn the pink in her cheeks to a deep carnation and felt a flare of satisfaction.

'Listen to yourself!' she jeered shakily. 'Have you any idea what an arrogant idiot you sound? It was just a kiss and you're not *that* good.' Actually he was. 'Though I suppose we might see one another again if Annie and Connor get married—'

'Isn't going to happen,' he cut in harshly.

'Well, as you're *never* wrong…'

'Sarcastic little witch,' he countered, an appreciative grin lightening the brooding severity of his lean features.

'…This really is goodbye. The last time I'll see you, or be insulted by you or…' She stopped and shot him a look from under her lashes that was shining with wry amusement. 'I've just thought, if they do get married, will that make you my brother?'

'It bloody won't!' he ejaculated in an accent of revulsion.

'You think that being related to me would be *that* awful?' she demanded, hurt by his strong reaction to her joke.

'If you were my sister I couldn't do this.'

He jerked her to him forcefully even though there was no question that Lucy was going to offer any resistance. She wanted to breathe in the warm scent of his body and feel the controlled strength of his arms—she wanted him!

The moment their lips touched she melted. Her lips responded to the insistent pressure and parted. She moaned into his mouth as his tongue stabbed deep inside the warmth.

'Oh, God!' she breathed as she curved her arms around his neck and pressed herself up against the lean, vital length of him. The feelings being around him evoked crystallised into a hunger that was totally consuming.

When they drew apart she was shaking; she couldn't take her eyes off him.

The taut silence between them stretched and stretched.

'That felt as if you'd been thinking about it.' Her husky comment did not ease the tension, the air around them thick with it.

A fierce grin split his dark features. 'I was.' His eyelashes flickered lower. 'I am.'

Lucy swallowed as the heavy, dragging sensation low in her belly intensified. 'Me too.' Well, there goes mysterious and enigmatic.

'Listen would you like to go for a coffee? Or maybe—'

'No,' she interrupted. 'Not really.'

Finn's blue eyes grew blank as they slid away from hers. 'Right,' he murmured.

She watched him drag a hand through his hair and was hit by an almost overwhelming compulsion to do the same, let her fingers slide deep into the silky dark mass, trace the shape of his skull with her fingertips…

Lucy couldn't take her eyes off the wildly pulsing nerve in his lean cheek. This was her call; she could do this thing, take the initiative and stay in control. You do the propositioning, Lucy—you're in control. It made sense. You carry on believing that, the sarcastic voice in her head advised.

'But we could go to my place if you'd like.' She heard the brazen invitation but couldn't believe it had come from her own lips.

Well, I always wondered what it would feel like to bungee jump—now I know! Her stomach had shifted into her cramped chest cavity.

Something fierce that both excited and frightened her flared in his expressive eyes. *'I'd like,'* he rasped throatily.

She gave a fractured little gasp, no longer able to maintain the pretence that she propositioned extraordinarily handsome men every day of the week. Not that Finn could know that; as far as he was concerned she might do this sort of thing all the time. Should I tell him I don't or will that sound…?

Do you know what you're doing, Lucy?

Oh, God, I'm totally clueless!

It wasn't actually the *what* she had a problem with, it was the *why*. This is daylight, you're stone-cold sober…there are absolutely no extenuating circumstances to explain away such wanton behaviour.

'Right…this doesn't mean I'll help you with Annie and Connor. I still think you're totally wrong to interfere.'

He dismissed her words with a shrug. 'You know my views—'

'Well, you're hardly shy about voicing them, are you?'

Her sarcastic interruption brought an unapologetic, 'Well, for the record, they haven't changed.'

My God, the man was so damned full of himself, what had she thought she had seen in him? 'Well, maybe I've changed my mind about…'

'No, you haven't, Lucy.'

Lucy looked up into his darkly beautiful face and shivered. She shook her head. 'No,' she agreed huskily, 'I haven't.'

CHAPTER EIGHT

LIKE someone in a dream Lucy slipped off her jacket and let it fall in a crumpled heap to the floor. Underneath she just wore a lace camisole. The cool air on her hot skin was welcome. She lifted her hair from her neck and sighed.

She opened her eyes and saw him standing there, watching her. His eyes had been on her small, pointed breasts that strained against the thin fabric that barely covered them. Her heart battered against her ribcage, she could hardly breathe, but boldly she held his gaze.

'The guest bedroom isn't very big,' Lucy explained as she opened the door and led the way.

She was way past caring if she came over as some brazen bimbo who wanted to rip his clothes off. Actually it suited her pretty well if he thought of her that way. She might never be more than a casual conquest to Finn, but he was more than that to her...she didn't want to think about how much more, there would be time enough for that later.

She was shaking, her entire body hit by intermittent tremors over which she had absolutely no control. They'd started when she'd asked him to come home with her and had been getting gradually worse—or better, depending on how you looked at it!—as her state of heightened desire increased.

And it had!

When Finn had offered to pay him double if he got there in under ten the taxi driver had asked him if there was a fire. Finn had looked at her with a secret smile that made her dissolve and said, *'Kind of.'*

He hadn't taken her in his arms in the cab, he hadn't kissed her, or even touched her in any way, but he'd been close enough for her to hear every breath he took…smell the warm, musky, male scent of his body…feel the warmth of his skin…feel his breath stir the fine down on her cheek.

It had been the most effective form of torture Lucy could imagine anyone devising. There was only so much stimulation a girl could take before she snapped and Lucy thought she might be close to that point.

She actually found herself wondering at one point, and not in a whimsical way, what the driver would say if she suddenly demanded he pull over so that she could take advantage of the man beside her. There were bus lanes and bike lanes, the fact there was no designated lane for people who couldn't wait until they got home was a major oversight that could be a vote-winner for future mayoral candidates!

By the time the journey came to an end Lucy had sweated off several pounds, would have been classed as certifiably insane in some countries and was so aroused, so *consumed* by her need for him that she was totally incapable of speech, let alone pretending to make intelligent responses to the things he was saying—how did he do that? Maybe he didn't feel the same, maybe he had control or even had lost interest. A moment's contact with the smouldering desire in his incredible eyes had zapped that theory.

'Well, actually, it's more of a box room,' she admitted, kicking a pair of shoes under the divan and turning around.

Finn's chest was about an inch from her nose; resisting the desire to burrow herself up against that hardness, that warmth, made her head spin.

Would the reality be a bit of an anticlimax after all this build-up…?

'Do you honestly think I care?'

Lucy shivered and closed her eyes, her head falling back as he ran a finger down her neck.

'I'm just making conversation,' she admitted throatily.

'I'd prefer to make love.'

She lifted her eyes to his and the raw, unvarnished need she saw shining there paralysed her with longing. With a low, keening cry she suddenly pressed her face into his shirt front. Her hands fought for purchase on the hard-muscled contours of his broad back to draw him closer. Listening to the heavy thud of his heartbeat, she gave a tiny sigh of relief.

Finn took her face between his hands and looked wonderingly down into her eyes.

'I can't believe that twelve hours ago I didn't know your name. I had never kissed those lips.' His already unsteady voice thickened as his eyes dwelt on the soft, quivering curves of her full mouth. 'I had never smelt this hair.' He buried his head in the pale strands of hair covering her head before watching the silky strands slip through his brown fingers. 'I didn't even know you existed!' he breathed incredulously.

A shudder of horror slid down her spine. 'That would have been a shame.'

'*A shame?*' he spat out, pulling her hard against him so that she could feel the strength of his arousal pulse into the softness of her stomach. 'Tragedy, more like,' he groaned. 'I've never wanted a woman the way I want you, Lucy.' His insolent smile of sexual confidence wavered as he realised he meant *exactly* what he'd just said.

'I want you too, Finn,' she replied simply, too involved in what she was feeling to see the shock of discovery on his face. 'So very much.'

Finn's nostrils flared as he inhaled deeply and angled his head so that he could seal his mouth to hers. Lucy trembled and clung to him as his tongue slid smoothly between her parted lips, probing deep into the moist, warm interior.

With his mouth still sealed to hers, he picked her up as though she weighed nothing and carried her to the narrow bed, where he tenderly laid her down.

He just stood looking down at her, his eyes dark with desire.

Her eyelids quivered but did not lift, her breath emerged through her slightly parted lips in noisy little whimpers. Each detail fascinated him.

Lucy felt the mattress move as Finn disposed his long length beside her. The knot of hot excitement in her belly expanded until her entire body was consumed by the flame. She waited in a state of almost painful arousal for his next move.

There was a tremor in the strong fingers that began to work loose the straps of her camisole, and then as she felt him slip them down her shoulders she relaxed.

Finn held his breath as he peeled back the silky covering and revealed her firm breasts. Then inhaled sharply as the soft, pink-tipped mounds sprang free from their confinement.

'Oh, my God, you're perfect…!'

Lucy felt her already distended nipples tingle and ache as they were exposed to the air. She sighed and flexed the tight muscles in her neck and shoulders, relishing the freedom. She lifted her heavy eyelids and looked at him with an expression of sultry invitation.

'You make me feel… Oh, God!' she breathed, her back arching. 'That is… Oh, God…!' she cried again, this time barely audible.

She looked at his brown hand curved over her breast and her mind went blank.

'I knew it would fit.' His eyes were on her face as he

took her distended nipple between his forefinger and thumb
and teased the hardened flesh, and the satisfaction and fas-
cination in his eyes intensified as a low, almost feral moan
emerged from her lips.

Her head thrashed back and forth on the pillow, a stream
of disjointed admonitions emerging from her mouth as lips
and tongue began to explore the area his fingers had already
become familiar with.

Just when she didn't think she could bear it any longer
she felt his fingers slide under the waistband of her skirt.
She lifted her hips to assist him as he pulled it over her
hips.

Yesterday even *imagining* herself in a situation where
she was lying there in just a pair of pants and lacy-topped
hold-up stockings would have reduced her to a stiff bundle
of painful inhibitions.

Now here she was doing it for real, and there wasn't an
inhibition in sight. What was it about this man that made
her behave with such shameless…no, *delicious* wanton
abandon?

She felt his mouth touch the soft flesh of her gently
rounded belly and such questions became irrelevant. The
tide of sensation that washed over her was so intense she
didn't think she could bear it but each time she thought this
he touched her in a new and marvellous way.

By the time he began kissing her mouth again Lucy was
in a state of mindless hunger. Every sense stretched, every
taut muscle begging for release, she was aware of her own
body and its needs in a way she never had been before.

'I want to see you,' she heard herself say.

For a moment Finn's eyes blazed down into hers then
without a word he got up. Still holding her passion-glazed
eyes, he began to remove his clothes.

He was beautiful; as each fresh item of clothing joined

the growing pile on the floor it became clear just how beautiful. Within moments he stood there magnificently unselfconscious in his nakedness. And more beautiful than she had imagined a man could be.

She wanted him more than she had ever wanted anything in her life.

The sound of the blood pounding in Finn's head became deafening when she slowly parted her thighs in invitation. He could see the soft, downy hair peeking through the light, lacy covering of the provocative pants. But it was her awed gasp when her eyes saw the effect her actions had on his already painfully aroused body that made him lose the last shreds of his control.

Need was etched on his dark features as he moved over her, his weight braced on his elbows.

'You're so beautiful,' he breathed into her mouth. 'Made for me.'

Lucy heard the lacy fabric of her pants rip as they came apart in his hands. A low moan vibrated in his throat as he felt how ready she was for him.

When he finally slid into her, Lucy's entire body jolted as if she'd been hit by lightning. Then slowly, blissfully, as he began to rock up into her every individual cell in her body relaxed and went with him.

'Oh, God!' she cried, gripping on to his brown shoulders as new tension built within her, one that was nothing like she'd ever experienced. When that tension finally splintered she dissolved as she hit a wall of pure pleasure.

Mere seconds after the muscles deep in her abdomen first began to convulse she felt him shudder above her and cry out. It was only then that Lucy realised that she was crying out too, she was crying his name over and over.

*   *   *

The noise immediately woke Finn, who was a light sleeper.

'What's that?' the figure in his arms demanded sleepily before burrowing into his shoulder.

Finn, his movements restricted by the warm, relaxed body that lay on top of his own, brushed the soft strands of silky hair from her forehead, and an expression of extraordinary tenderness softened the hard lines of his lean face as he watched her eyelashes flutter against the curve of her cheek before stilling.

'It's nothing; go to sleep, sweetheart.'

The tension left his neck when the noise stopped, and he cursed quietly when it started up again almost immediately. With infinite care Finn disentangled their limbs, his arms supporting her supine body as he slid from underneath her before lowering her still sleeping form onto the mattress. Lastly he slid his arm from under Lucy's shoulders.

Eyes closed, she reached blindly out for him. Finn caught her hand and pressed it to his lips, his eyes darkening.

'I'll be back,' he promised, his lips brushing her ear.

Finn watched as a smile curved her soft lips before she turned over and went back to sleep.

He had found himself incredibly reluctant to move away from the fragrant warmth of her soft body. The reluctance he felt to leave the warm bed was not something he was accustomed to; even more alien was the fiercely protective feeling he experienced as he looked down at the figure lying there.

Vulnerable in repose, her face had the rosy glow of sleep, pink lips slightly parted. He felt his libido stir and briefly allowed himself to imagine waking her before deliberately turning away—he wasn't a kid, he had control—from the temptation offered by her mouth.

An image flashed in his head of her beneath him, her lips parted, her pale body drenched in sweat, each muscle and tendon stretched as she approached the climax that had convulsed her.

It took all of the self-control that he was so smug about to get out of that room.

As he reached the phone the answer machine kicked in.

'Lucy, I need to talk to you—please pick up if you're there… I'll ring back later or, better still, ring me; we're staying near Keswick at the Grange. Did I give you the number?' Finn stood there as the disembodied female voice at the other end of the line reeled off a number.

There was a gap of several seconds after the voice had died away before Finn reached for the pad and pen beside the phone and began to jot down a number. Nothing about his manner suggested triumph.

Lucy woke to the sound of a pneumatic drill somewhere on the street below. It didn't have the romantic potential of a dawn chorus, but who needed props…?

It was strange to wake up beside someone, knowing that all she had to do was turn over and…? The anticipation of what would happen when she did brought a flush to her cheeks.

She lay there motionless for several minutes, not because she was embarrassed or apprehensive about the morning-after thing—how could you feel awkward when what had gone before had felt so natural and perfect…? She just wanted some time to marvel at the wonderful newness of the situation.

What would Finn do when he woke and saw her…? If he showed the same recuperative powers and insatiability he had the night before…maybe she wouldn't wait for him to wake, maybe she would wake him. She laughed softly at her own brazen impatience, and with a sultry smile she rolled over, taking the covers with her.

The corners of her mouth drooped when she didn't discover the dark head she had anticipated on the pillow beside her. Feeling a nasty sense of anticlimax but at that stage no premonition of unpleasant surprises to come, she rolled onto her stomach and wondered if she should wait or go and find him.

It took her about three seconds to come to a decision.

She paused only long enough to slip on a robe before opening the door and calling his name. She continued to do so as she walked through the flat…it was several minutes before she realised Finn wasn't going to answer because Finn wasn't there.

He'd slipped away before she had woken without even leaving a note…note—of course, why hadn't she thought of that? Finn hadn't wanted to disturb her and he… *You're making excuses for the guy.*

'No! No, I'm not!'

She saw the note propped up on the mantel shelf and gave a sigh of relief. Snatching it up, she unfolded the paper and read the note. It was brief and to the point.

I picked up a message your sister left on the machine. I'm going to find out what Con's playing at. I know you'll be mad but once I get this sorted we can concentrate on us.

Lucy stood motionless for several minutes, then with vicious precision she ripped the note into confetti and let it fall to the floor.

'There is no us.' Her voice was like stone in the empty room; in her breast she felt just as heavy and cold. She had thought it meant something to him—thought it was something special for him. She cringed at her stupidity.

*   *   *

Lucy was pounding away furiously on the laptop and didn't hear the door open.

'You're writing…? That's good.'

'Annie!' Lucy leapt up from the chair, deeply alarmed by her sister's unhealthy pallor and the total lack of expression on her face. 'I didn't expect you back until tomorrow…?'

'I didn't expect to be b…back.' Annie's flat, emotionless voice broke on the last word. Her face crumpled. 'Oh, God, Lucy, I want to die…!'

Lucy immediately ran to enfold her sister in a warm embrace. 'Don't cry, Annie he's not worth it; none of them is,' she remarked viciously.

'Con's worth it,' Annie sobbed into her shoulder. 'I love him!' she wailed.

Lucy felt helpless in the face of such misery. 'This is Finn's doing.' She awkwardly patted her sister's head. 'But don't worry, I'll make him sorry.' Her eyes narrowed to slits. 'If it's the last thing I do I'll…'

Annie's tear-stained face lifted from Lucy's shoulder. '*Finn?* Oh, you mean Con's brother; why should this have anything to do with him? I've never even met him. No, it's C…Con…' Her lower lip wobbled as her voice once more became suspended by tears.

Ironically it seemed that Finn's intervention hadn't been needed at all.

'What did Con do, Annie?' Lucy prompted gently when after several minutes there had been no let-up in the unrestrained weeping.

'It's too awful!' Annie told her in a muffled whisper.

Lucy's alarm deepened. 'You can tell me.' Nothing could be as bad as the things she was imagining.

Sniffing and wiping her wet face with the back of her hand, Annie nodded and straightened up. 'I'm all right now,' she said, detaching herself from her sister and collapsing gracefully—Annie did everything gracefully—into an armchair.

'Have you got a tissue?' she asked with a watery grin. She nodded her thanks when Lucy produced a wad. 'Sorry about that, but on the train back I wanted to cry but I couldn't...'

'Don't apologise,' Lucy said, perching herself on the arm of the chair and stroking her sister's hair. 'Did you find out about him being married twice before?' she asked sympathetically.

'God, no, I knew about that from the beginning.'

'Oh!'

'Con was very open about it.'

'Then?'

'He proposed.'

'Oh...' Lucy nodded understandingly. 'And he got nasty when you said no. As if you'd marry someone after knowing them for a few weeks...' she scoffed.

'I said yes, Lucy,' Annie said quietly.

Lucy's mouth fell open; she swallowed. 'Right...yes...'

'That was the first night; it was incredibly romantic,' Annie recalled dreamily. 'Dinner in our room, candles, soft music and then later on...' She lowered her gaze, blushing prettily. 'Well, let's just say it was worth the wait, if you see what I mean.'

Lucy, who felt herself blush, did. 'Then what went wrong?'

The soft light faded from Annie's eyes as she wrapped her arms about herself as if she was cold. 'This morning,' she recalled in a bewildered voice, 'I woke up and Con wasn't there...'

Déjà vu.

Annie looked up questioningly at the strangled sound that escaped Lucy's lips.

Lucy smiled stiffly and shook her head. 'Nothing.'

Maybe Annie was finding the whole post-mortem thing cathartic but Lucy didn't think it would work that way with her. The wounds were too fresh and she wasn't ready to share her humiliating experiences with anyone.

'When I found him he was sitting on the balcony; I knew right off something was wrong—he looked so distant, so cold. He said…he said a lot actually, but to summarise he said he couldn't marry me…he loved me, but he couldn't m…marry me…' The tears welled from under her closed eyelids as her shoulders began to heave.

Lucy frowned in bewilderment. 'But why?'

'I don't know why…I hate him…!' Annie snarled. 'No, I don't, I love him… You must think I'm mad.'

'No, Annie, I know exactly how you feel.'

'Lucy…?'

'Yes.'

Annie gave a forlorn sniff, her frown deepening as she tried to sort out a puzzling inconsistency. 'How did you know Con had been married, and for that matter how did you know his brother's name?'

'Oh, he dropped by looking for Con.'

'Really? And I forgot to leave you a number. They were brought up apart, you know,' she said, blowing her nose loudly. 'Con stayed with his dad and Finn went with their mother—I think Con still feels his mother rejected him, you know, choosing Finn over him.'

'That's not Finn's fault.'

'Oh, Con doesn't blame him, he only says good things about his brother, and anyhow by all accounts Con got the better deal, not that you'd know it to hear him talk. I think

it's because Finn has done so much more than he has...'
she mused.

Lucy was relieved that Annie didn't seem to have noticed
how she had automatically sprung to Finn's defence at the
first suggestion of criticism—*what is wrong with me? The
guy's a rat! And, worse, he's a user!*

'I don't expect he'd think it was quite so glamorous to
live in all those exciting places—Los Angeles, New York,
Chicago—if he'd been the one who never stayed long
enough in a school to make friends.'

Lucy shook her head, picturing a younger Finn never
staying in one place long enough to call it home, leading
a gypsy existence. 'No, I don't suppose he would.'

'And can you imagine having four stepdads in the space
of ten years?

Four! 'No.' The way Finn compartmentalised his life
made a sort of sense. He wasn't going to put his son
through what he had experienced by allowing him to get
fond of women who were only a temporary part of his life.

'How did he strike you?'

'Who?' Lucy played for time, immensely relieved that
her sister wasn't looking at her when she'd asked that question.

'Finn; Con thinks he's brilliant, really admires him and
says he's the most together person he knows.'

'Oh, I'd say Finn would be the first to agree with that.'

This drew a weak laugh from Annie. 'Tell me, do you
think it's my fault...? Perhaps I was terrible in—'

'That is such a woman thing to do!' Lucy cut in, throwing her hands up in exasperation. 'Never, ever, let me hear
you say that again, Annie Foster. Promise?'

'Promise.'

CHAPTER NINE

KEYS caught between her teeth, arms full of bulging carrier bags, Lucy pushed the front door of the flat wider with her bottom before backing into the hallway.

'Annie!'

There was only silence in reply. Annie must have decided to go for a drink with the old friend who was in town after all. Lucy was glad she'd changed her mind; in her opinion it was about time her sister stopped moping at home—time she got back into the social swing and forgot about Connor Fitzgerald.

The way you've forgotten about his big brother? the voice in her head suggested slyly.

It was true that Annie wasn't the only one struggling to get over a Fitzgerald male, but Annie's response had been very different from her own.

Lucy's smooth brow wrinkled in concern as she considered Annie's behaviour, she hated to see her animated sister act as though nothing mattered. Oh, she kept up appearances when anyone else was there, or she was at work, but when they were at home Annie could barely summon the energy to get dressed, and she wasn't eating either. Lucy hated to see the drawn, haggard look on her face.

She, on the other hand, had gone into overdrive.

Working on the theory that if she filled every moment with frenetic activity she wouldn't have time to think, *this hadn't been an unqualified success*. The upside was that she had done more of her novel during the past week than she had over the entire preceding six months.

So maybe it was right what they said about dark clouds and silver linings.

People lived without sex, *she* could live without sex, she had proved it, and there had been nothing more than that between her and Finn—a sexual attraction. To suggest there had been anything deeper and more profound was absurd, and suggesting there was no gap in her life to fill, that was just plain daft.

Finn Fitzgerald was a mistake, nothing more.

You carry on telling yourself that, girl. You never know, you might even start to believe it!

Propping the heavy grocery bags containing amongst other things the ingredients for her sister's favourite Thai dish against the wall, Lucy clicked the front door shut with a frown.

It actually didn't seem to matter how hard she tried not to, she mused, or for that matter how much she tried to divert herself by filling every second of the day, the truth was she couldn't seem to go more than a few minutes without Finn Fitzgerald insinuating himself into her thoughts.

Maybe, she mused, that was the problem—she was trying *too* hard?

She dismissed the possibility almost instantly; the idea of lowering her defences was not an option she was prepared to seriously consider. She would get through this, she told herself—*she had to*!

Keeping busy was some help, she only had to consider the empty night-time hours for proof of this, so taking over the cooking and cleaning in the flat not only made her feel as if she was contributing something but it also left her less time to think about Finn.

As the days went by she was getting more concerned about the extended length of her stay with Annie. So she was cooking; that hardly represented a major contribution, and had her sister known how critically low Lucy's financial reserves were she would have been even more reluctant to accept the little Lucy was kicking into the joint finances.

Lucy was grimly determined not to sponge off Annie, but she knew that if she didn't get a job of some sort her only other choice would be to go back home. And, though she knew her recently married mother would never say so, a grown-up daughter living under her roof would cramp her style. After a long and lonely widowhood when she had put the needs of her daughters ahead of her own, Lucy reckoned it was time her mum put herself first—something she knew she wouldn't do if she suspected for an instant that one of her precious children needed her help.

For this reason the sisters had colluded in inventing a marvellous job which Lucy had been offered. Lucy felt incredibly guilty about the deception, but she was grimly determined to get a job so that their mum would never need to know about the lie.

A frown of determination brought a furrow to her smooth brow as she ran a hand through her hair to remove the excess of moisture—the summer shower she had been caught in had been short but heavy. She grimaced; her T-shirt was clinging uncomfortably to her back and there were dark stains of dampness on her jeans—she couldn't wait to get out of them and into the shower.

Arms crossed, she took hold of the soggy cotton hem and pulled the clinging T-shirt over her head before heading for the bathroom. Dumping it in the linen basket, she snatched up a towel off the heated rail and after rubbing her damp skin she began to blot the moisture out of her hair. The shower beckoned but first things first, she needed to unpack the perishables.

Humming softly under her breath, Lucy headed back to the hall with the damp towel looped around her neck. As she picked up the supermarket carrier bags which had left a pool of water on the wooden floor her thoughts turned to the problem of her employment situation, a problem which she might just have solved in the short term, though Annie would hit the roof when she found out.

Where had Annie got her snobby streak from?

Lucy been chatting to the girl at the checkout when the other girl had happened to mention about how short-staffed they were with several women on maternity leave. An enquiry at the manager's office had confirmed they were looking for part-time temporary staff and she had come home with the application forms.

So it was all done and dusted, barring Annie's inevitable complaints that she was lowering her sights and working in a supermarket was a waste of a good degree.

'Here, let me help you.'

Unexpectedly relieved of the bulk of her burdens, Lucy found herself looking directly into the unmistakable iridescent blue eyes of Finn Fitzgerald. The rest of her bundles slipped from her nerveless fingers and fell unnoticed to the floor. If she had been attached to a cardiac monitor they would have been screaming for the crash team!

'*You!*' she cried out in a voice that ached with loathing.

'You didn't answer my calls or reply to my messages.'

'So you decided to try the personal touch after how long, ten days?' *God, that makes it sound as though I've been counting.* 'What's wrong, Finn, have you a night free and you thought, well, why not call in on Lucy—she'll have nothing better to do and she's a sure thing…?'

His eyes darkened with anger. 'Don't talk about yourself that way—I don't like it,' he rasped.

'And that means *so* much to me.'

His nostrils flared as he struggled quite obviously to control his temper. 'I've been out of the country. It's not as if I haven't been calling.'

'I unplugged the phone.'

'I explained everything in my letters.' Two a day.

'I didn't open them.'

He dragged a hand through his sleek dark hair. 'Don't you think that was slightly childish…?'

'Childish…! Have you any idea what it feels like to wake up and find the man you spent the night with wasn't after your body but an address? I think I'd have preferred it if you'd stolen my purse. No, I *know* I'd have preferred it.'

Finn flinched at the depth of feeling in her derisive retort. 'I left a note.'

The tone in his voice that suggested she was being irrational made her flip.

'Oh, yes, the note.' Her eyes narrowed to glittering slits. 'I wish I'd kept that note so I could have watched you eat it!' She ended on a quivering note of outrage.

'I was in a hurry.'

'Yes, to save your brother from my sister.'

An inscrutable expression on his tense, lean features, Finn gazed down into her angry golden eyes. 'That isn't relevant.'

'Want to bet?'

'You can't possibly think I spent the night with you for any other reason but…' He broke off, a frustrated expression on his face.

'But what, Finn?'

A ragged laugh was wrenched from him; the raw explanation seemed drawn equally unwillingly. 'I couldn't not!' he ground out. 'You want to know why I didn't wake you that morning? Because I knew that if you looked at me I'd have to spend the rest of the day making love to you.'

A soundless hiss escaped through Lucy's parted lips as

her insides melted. I won't let him do this to me again, I won't!

'You see, I have absolutely no self-control where you're concerned. No woman has ever affected me the way you do...'

The harsh, uneven rasp of his voice did terrible, exciting things to her, and as for the burning light of raw, unvarnished hunger in his stunning eyes... Breaking the spell that paralysed her vocal cords and pinned her feet to the ground required a superhuman effort that left her sweating.

'How did you get in here?' She looked around wildly. 'And what have you done with my sister?'

Finn gave a twisted smile; the scenario where she'd throw herself into his arms had always been a long shot...but for a moment there she'd wanted to... 'You mean, where have I put the body?'

The satiric lash of his words brought a dark flush to her pale cheeks.

'I wouldn't put anything past you.'

Lucy despised the weakness in herself that made her eat up details of his appearance. Everything about him was the way she remembered it, only more so—the intense blue of his eyes was even bluer, the lean power of his streamlined body more sharply defined and the aura of raw sexuality he projected more tangible.

It was this last quality that made her mind go blank—so no change there.

In strong contrast to herself Finn was in total control. There was no sheen of sweat on his healthy, toned skin and she seriously doubted his mouth was dry or his knees shaking. Despite the effect he *claimed* she had on him, he was looking at her as though she was a casual acquaintance, which she supposed she was—a casual acquaintance, he had just happened to have sex with!

Maybe one day she would be able to consider that event a bitter-sweet memory, but right now it was just *bitter*!

Finn's sardonic expression softened abruptly as he scanned her pale face, sensing the deep distress behind the hostility.

'I would think,' he glanced at the discreet but expensive watch on his wrist, 'that Annie is at this moment enjoying a drink with a friend. She invited me in.' One brow lifted as a scornful snort escaped through Lucy's clenched teeth. 'And then she very kindly allowed me to wait here for you.'

As she listened to his explanation the knots of painful anxiety in Lucy's stomach tightened. There was a disbelieving silence before she shook her head, refusing to believe Annie would betray her that way.

'My sister wouldn't do that…she wouldn't even open the door to you.' She grimaced to hear the weak note of uncertainty enter her quavery voice.

'Believe what you like, but I'm here.'

As if she needed reminding when every cell in her body was acutely and painfully aware of him.

'Feel if you don't believe me,' he suggested, holding his arms wide in open invitation.

Lucy stared at his shirt front; she knew that the faint darker shadows showing through the fine fabric of his shirt were actually strategic drifts of dark hair across his chest. She knew that if she did touch him he would feel lean and hard…and she wouldn't want to stop… She dragged her eyes back to his face.

'I'll pass.'

Finn's hands fell to his sides, but his sardonic smile left Lucy with the mortifying conviction that he knew exactly how difficult it had been for her to refuse his invitation.

'I don't know how you talked your way in here,' she interposed, determined to emulate his self-possession if it killed her, which it probably would, she thought, dabbing the tip of her tongue to the beads of sweat that had sprung up along her upper lip, 'what lies you told Annie, but you can go now.' She grabbed the bags from his arms and dropped them in a messy heap on the floor.

'After I've said what I came to say,' he returned, his cool demeanour unaffected by the animosity shimmering in her topaz eyes.

'I thought you already had; you've explained you didn't wake me up because it would have messed up your schedule.'

This gross misinterpretation of something that he'd had a hard time admitting brought a flash of anger to Finn's lean face. 'I didn't say anything of the sort.'

'So I was reading between the lines…oh, and I forgot it was mostly my fault anyhow for inspiring blind lust. Being seductive is such a curse…' she bemoaned.

Finn's facial muscles clenched tight as he took a deep, angry breath that lifted his chest and sucked in his abdominal muscles tight.

Lucy would have liked nothing better than to believe the sight of her first thing in the morning could drive a man wild with uncontrollable lust—what woman wouldn't? But she had a mirror! And he was Finn, who was the most heartbreakingly beautiful man alive…she just couldn't accept someone that looked like him wanted her that much. She had let herself believe it for a while, but she was herself again now.

She was sane; unhappy but sane.

'Actually, *nothing* you can say could possibly ever be of interest to me.' She gave a regal toss of her head but the effect was rather spoilt when the motion sent damp strands of her hair across her face.

'It's raining outside?' Finn said, his eyes on the silvered drops of moisture that shone on her rain-darkened hair.

He knew that if he took her in his arms she would smell of rain and summer. The effort of not testing this theory was making him sweat; he could feel the dampness on the palms of his hands and the rivulets of moisture running down his back. Women didn't make him sweat, he just wasn't into all that emotional turbulence. Maybe he was coming down with that summer cold that was around.

Sure you are, Finn!

She'd wanted an opportunity to tell him what she thought of him, and now she'd done that she ought to be feeling better, but she wasn't. Unless a sense of closure was meant to make you feel wretchedly unhappy.

'Just say what you need to and go,' she suggested wearily.

'I thought you weren't interested in anything I've got to say.'

'Don't be so pedantic,' she sniffed.

'Then you *are* interested in what I say.'

'I'm not! But if it's the only way to get rid of you...' She gave an eloquent shrug. 'In case you missed the point, Finn, these are precious seconds of my life I won't be getting back and I can think of things I'd prefer to be doing—interesting things like watching paint dry...so could you get to the point?'

Finn winced. 'I'm reading here—don't hesitate to correct me if I'm wrong—that we won't be taking off where we left off...relationship-wise that is. Why,' he asked with a puzzled frown when she snorted, 'do you keep making that noise?'

'I keep making that noise because I simply don't believe you. You have to be the most arrogant, egocentric—' she broke off and took several deep, steadying breaths before explaining how things were.

'Firstly, we will not be taking up where we left off. Secondly, we did not have a relationship…' she swallowed, feeling the heat mount in her cheeks '…you had sex with me because your schedule was free and you wanted to find out where your brother and my sister were—and it worked. Congratulations,' she ended bitterly.

His eyes darkened in a way that made Lucy's hopelessly sensitive stomach flip. 'That is not why I slept with you, Lucy.'

'Then why did…? Actually, don't answer that!' She held up her hand; she couldn't bear to hear his slick lies, especially as she might be crazy enough to swallow them. 'Have it your way,' she added huskily. 'And we'll pretend it was just a happy coincidence that it worked out that way.'

She turned her head away, afraid that he would be able to see in her face how much she had *not* come to terms with being used. Lucy didn't think she could cope if Finn began to suspect that it had not been casual for her.

'Why are you acting as if you hate me when we both know you don't? Look at me and tell me a single second of the day goes by without you thinking about me…about us,' he challenged, in a low, intense voice that really shook Lucy.

'I don't hate you, Finn, I despise you,' she shot back coldly.

Something angry moved in his eyes but he didn't respond to her declaration. Instead he shifted his attention to the bags around her feet, which had spilled their contents over the floor.

'The food might spoil—perhaps we should put it away first,' he suggested.

Now, doesn't that just say it all? she thought bitterly.

There she was, hardly able to think straight for the lustful images of smooth golden skin and perfectly formed muscles, while all he bothered about was perishable goods!

If it wasn't so tragically pathetic she'd have laughed. It was bad enough that she was going to spend the rest of her life comparing future lovers with that experience—with him! But for him to act as if he was just some innocent victim of circumstance, that was the limit! And as for suggesting that she would carry on as if nothing had happened…

'You won't be here long enough for anything to spoil.'

Finn watched a convulsive shiver run through her body. 'You know, you should get some clothes on.' He doubted his offer of assistance would be warmly received.

Lucy's attempt to read his expression was frustrated by the concealing dark fringe of his eyelashes as his eyes remained focused on her body.

Horror washed over her as she grasped the significance of his advice to get some clothes on—she wasn't wearing any!

With a shriek of shock she looked down and for several moments she remained frozen with horror. Then as her paralysis lost its grip she clasped one arm protectively across her chest, hiding the scraps of pink lace through which the deeper shade of her nipples was clearly visible.

What he had seen made it impossible for her to pretend certain things weren't happening, the most significant and disturbing of which were the aching heaviness of her breasts and the brazen thrust of her engorged nipples. She rubbed her free hand nervously over her thighs, where she felt the heaviness of the wet denim that was already becoming cold against her skin.

'Your concern for my welfare is touching…' she began huskily.

'Actually it's my concentration I'm more concerned about,' he responded with a self-derisive twist of his lips. 'That is really a very provocative outfit.'

'You knew I'd forgotten,' she accused hotly.

'Because seeing me drove every other consideration from your mind…?'

Lucy bit back a retort, not to deprive him of the satisfaction of debating a subject that was deeply embarrassing but because she recognised she was on extremely dangerous ground.

'Like I said, if you've got something to say, Finn, say it,' she recommended tautly.

'I understand from your sister that you've not had any luck on the job front yet?'

Lucy could not hide her shocked response to his remark, which strongly suggested he had enjoyed a cosy little chat with Annie. What had Annie been thinking about? Too busy admiring his blue eyes to think at all probably, she thought sourly. When she saw her big sister she'd have a lot to say about discretion…that wasn't important now, she told herself; *focus…focus*. The question now was, just what else had Annie told him?

'There are several possibilities I'm considering.' Including hysterics in the short term.

Finn stifled a surge of exasperation as he cast appraising eyes over her slim, defiant figure. Arms crossed over her chest, she was literally dithering with cold, but she was too stubborn and pigheaded to do anything sensible such as get into some dry clothes simply because he was the one who had suggested it.

'I'd prefer to talk to you somewhere I'm less likely to hit my head.' To illustrate his point he ducked under the low pendant light and headed back towards the sitting room.

Lucy took the opportunity to head for her bedroom, unhooking her wet bra as she knelt down and pulling her suitcase out from under the bed. There was no space to spare in the cramped conditions of Annie's guest room for a wardrobe or chest of drawers, so apart from a few items which were on a small hanging rail the rest of Lucy's clothes were still in her suitcase.

Lucy entered the room breathlessly about two minutes later dressed in a dry pair of jeans and a black high-necked sleeveless T-shirt that clung to the pert outline of her small, high breasts and showed off the shapely line of shoulders and upper arms.

Finn, who had been looking out of the window to the narrow, congested street below, turned when she entered. Silently he took in the details of her appearance from the damp hair that clung to her cheeks and neck to her inevitable bare feet.

'I think you forgot your bra. You didn't need to hurry on my account. Or was it a deliberate choice…?' He gave a twisted smile.

It became a matter of pride not to react to his taunt. It became a matter of self-preservation not to look directly into his glittering eyes.

'Well, you know what they say—if you've got it, flaunt it.'

Her defiance brought an admiring smile to his wide, sensual mouth. 'Or is this in fact *not* about sex…?'

'You think everything is about sex!' she flung angrily.

His smile died. 'Everything between us is about sex.'

Lucy looked away, irrationally wounded by his comment, but at the same time excited by his words.

It wasn't as if she had ever *really* thought he cared about her, that she meant anything to him. She was just the woman he wanted in his bed—at least he did at the moment.

'Or were you in fact worried about leaving me alone with the family silver?' he wondered.

Well, if Annie had any it would be on show.

One of the first things Lucy's gaze had lit upon when she'd entered the room—after Finn—was a distinctive bone-china teacup from the set Annie had inherited from a great-aunt. The set that after an insurance valuation her financially astute sister had declared too valuable to be used.

Lucy's suggestion that half the pleasure of having beautiful things was using them had been declared ridiculously sentimental. Now there was this too-good-to-use antique sitting on the coffee-table.

It was difficult enough for her to accept that Annie had inexplicably invited him in, but now it seemed clear she had given him the VIP treatment too! Finn must have made quite an impression, she thought bitterly... Oh, God, now he's got me feeling jealous of my own sister!

'Do you mind?' Finn asked as he flicked on the gas fire set in the Victorian tiled fireplace.

'Would it matter if I did?'

'I've just got back from a short trip to California; I'm feeling the cold.'

He didn't look as if he was feeling the cold but she, on the other hand, was rather glad of the blast of heat. She hugged her arms a little tighter across her chest.

'To top up your tan?' The taunt unfortunately reminded her that there were no demarcation lines on his body...the glowing golden colour extended to parts the sun didn't get to see.

'Business,' he returned shortly. 'An unexpected opportunity—'

'Say no more,' she cut in with savage sarcasm. 'We all know that you can't resist an opportunity.'

'Neither can you, it seems, to twist the knife.'

'I didn't invite you here...' she reminded him with a sullen smile. 'Why *are* you here, Finn? You got what you wanted, your brother is safe and single...'

'I had nothing to do with what happened; that was up to them.'

'It didn't sound from what Annie told me that she had much to say about it,' she retorted indignantly.

'Maybe,' Finn conceded. 'But she was long gone before I even got to the hotel.' All he had discovered was his brother, who had been in a dangerously volatile state of mind.

One moment Connor had been congratulating himself that he had done the right thing and the next he had been in the depths of black despair, ranting that he had thrown away his one shot at true happiness.

Finn, who had never seen his brother this freaked out, had done what was required of him and listened...there hadn't been much else he could do. By the morning Con had been dejected but calmer.

'What do you think I should do, Finn?'

Now was his chance and what did he say...?

'I can't tell you what to do, Con; it has to be your decision.'

The confused look on Con's face made him wonder...did his brother rely too heavily on his judgement...was he over-protective? Finn put the blame for these sudden doubts where they belonged, squarely at Lucy Foster's door.

Someone who had ever considered getting married to Rupert Drake was in no position to stand as judge and jury on other people's actions and the next time she subjected his actions to critical scrutiny he was going to point this out to her.

'Yes, but do *you* think I'm doing the right thing?' Con persisted. 'I mean, *you'd* never propose to someone you'd only known for a few weeks, would you?' He laughed softly at the idea, oblivious to the fact his brother was looking as though he'd just been struck from behind by a large blunt object. 'You can't decide your future on a physical attraction—that's been my mistake. I see long legs and blonde hair and...not that Annie has long legs—nice legs but not long—and she's a redhead...'

'Listen, Con, maybe you should give yourself some time to think this thing through...?'

'There's nothing to think about.'

Lucy remembered their previous conversation. 'But if she had been there you'd have done everything in your power to split them up, wouldn't you?'

He appeared inexplicably amused by her accusation. 'You'd think so wouldn't you?'

'I *know* so,' she shouted angrily.

'Your sister seems to have accepted the situation more philosophically than you have,' he observed, scanning her stormy face.

Philosophically!

It was his extraordinary complacency that goaded her into indiscretion. 'I hear her crying herself to sleep every night.'

Finn's dark brows drew together as a flicker of shock crossed his dark face. It was some small comfort to Lucy to know she had put it there.

'*Surely not?*' The girl he had met had impressed him with her practical attitude.

'I've never seen Annie so shattered.'

Two bands of deep colour appeared along the sharp angles of his cheekbones as Finn read the total conviction in her blunt pronouncement.

'But she told me that she thought it was probably for the best in the long run...'

'And you swallowed it?' she demanded scornfully. 'Well, I suppose it was what you wanted to hear.' So far she and Annie had been pretty obliging. In her borrowed finery she had looked suitably unsuitable and Annie had said the things he wanted to hear. 'It makes you feel less guilty,' she charged scornfully.

'Interesting pop psychology, but I don't feel guilty. I don't have anything to feel guilty about.'

'Well, you should,' she declared furiously. 'Tell me, Finn, what did you *expect* her to say to *you*? Annie has pride.'

Something in which I seem sadly lacking, she thought in horrified realisation that the portion of her mind that wasn't involved in the verbal contest had even as she spoke been visualising pressing herself against the long, lean, beautiful lines of his body, breathing in the scent of his body, feeling his strong arms close about her.

She had to swallow several times to clear the emotional thickening in her throat before she continued.

'She's not the sort of person who enjoys being an object of pity, but take my word for it, underneath that bright, cheerful exterior she is hurting.' Her expression made it quite clear who she blamed for this situation.

'I'm sorry if your sister is unhappy; she seems a really nice person.'

'I thought your brother was only attracted to total bitches.'

'So did I.' An abstracted expression stole across his face as he looked into the distance. 'Maybe his tastes are maturing? It happens,' he said abruptly. 'Do you want tea? There's some in the pot.'

'I don't want tea, I want you out of here,' Lucy growled. 'So say what you came to say and get lost.'

Finn held her angry gaze for a moment longer before taking a seat in the armchair beside the flickering fake flames of the fire.

An image suddenly rose up in Lucy's head—an image so real she could feel his fingers running through her hair as she sat curled up at his feet, her head in his lap. It was the sound of her name that finally snapped her clear of the cosy fantasy image.

'Are you feeling all right, Lucy?'

Lucy resorted to a childish retort to hide the fact that the rough edge of unexpected tenderness in his voice had sliced cleanly through her already shredded defences.

'As all right as I could be *considering* the fact I'm breathing the same air as you…' she snarled.

Finn, supremely relaxed under attack, stretched his long legs out in front of him, their glances touched and locked. Without warning Lucy's topaz eyes filled.

'Well, what do you think…?'

Lucy blinked. 'About what?' she asked gruffly.

His eyes narrowed. 'Did you hear a *thing* I just said?'

'No…yes…' I was too busy lusting after you.

'I thought not. I asked you how you'd feel about working for me?'

Lucy sank into the nearest chair. She gave a strained laugh. 'Now tell me what you *really* came here for.'

'I have a son.' Finn's taut expression suggested his patience was wearing thin.

'I know, and no wife.' Because Finn Fitzgerald didn't need women outside the bedroom…

'I didn't come here to talk about Nina…'

Lucy seized eagerly on this evidence of his general slea-ziness—a man who could so carelessly dismiss the subject of the mother of his child was callous.

'Is she dead?' Lucy froze as she heard the appallingly indiscreet question slip from her tongue.

Finn looked taken aback but not particularly concerned. 'Of course she's not dead—anything but,' he added drily. 'She's working in Vegas. Whatever gave you the idea she was dead?'

'I don't know,' Lucy mumbled, deeply embarrassed. 'I suppose I just assumed because you're bringing up the baby alone...custody usually goes...'

'Liam isn't a baby, he's eight years old, and there was never any question of a custody battle,' he observed with a grim smile. 'And before your over-active imagination gets into gear I did not pressure Nina or use any form of coer-cion. Leaving Liam with me was entirely her choice.'

'I wasn't thinking anything of the sort,' she protested.

'You would have got there.'

'Then Liam was...' Something in his eyes made her stop before she said *accident*.

'I didn't plan to have a child with Nina,' he agreed qui-etly. 'But that doesn't mean he isn't a much wanted and much loved kid.'

Because there was no question of his sincerity Lucy was prepared to overlook the undercurrent of reprimand in his voice. Finn was obviously extremely protective of his son; even manipulative rats could love their kids, she thought, swallowing past the emotional constriction that had formed in her throat.

'I'm sure he is.' Despite her composed tone, her throat still ached as if she wanted to cry. 'Does he not see his mother at all?' If her inability to let the subject drop was puzzling Finn his ready reply to her clumsy probing was even more so.

'We decided that it would be too disruptive.'

'We or you?' The look he gave her made her blush. 'There are two sides to every story.'

'Well, in this story the ''mother'' thought it would be a good idea to get herself pregnant in order to snag herself a husband with some money. When she realised there was going to be no wedding ring she didn't want to go through with the pregnancy. So they reached an agreement...'

'Oh, that's...' Lucy gulped. 'Did you give her...?' That any woman could trade a baby as if it were a commodity shocked her deeply.

'I paid her to have the baby,' Finn confirmed. Unbelievably there was no trace of rancour in his voice. 'Part of our arrangement was the understanding that I would take full responsibility for the child.' His lips curved into an amused smile as he scanned her stricken face. 'You look shocked...not all women have maternal feelings, Lucy.'

'I don't suppose they do,' she agreed faintly.

Though Lucy had never thought much about her own maternal feelings, she could simply not imagine herself in a situation where she would give up her child to another person, even if that person was the father. But to do it for financial gain...!

At least the little boy had one parent who cared for him. Whatever else Finn lacked it was not a deep sense of parental responsibility.

'Well, do you want the job?'

CHAPTER TEN

UNABLE to believe what she was hearing, Lucy stared at him, her mouth slightly ajar.

'You were serious about that?' The proverbial feather wafted in her direction would have knocked her over at that moment.

'Isn't that what we've been talking about? Why else do you think I was entrusting private details about Liam's circumstances to you?' *Because you want her to think you're a nice guy,* he admitted to himself.

It was finally dawning on Lucy that this wasn't some sort of elaborate joke—Finn was serious. Her first impressions had been right—the man was unbalanced!

'What job are you offering me?'

'The job as my son's nanny.' Well, she hadn't rejected it outright. Actually she hadn't done anything, not even breathe as far as he could tell.

There was no harm knowing a few details of what she was going to refuse, Lucy told herself.

'You'd like the house,' he promised. 'It's in West Cork, and you have a view of the Irish sea from every window. We spend summer there. If you're worried about this being some elaborate scam to get you in my bed—'

'Oh, I'm not,' she cut in quickly.

'You're not?' His extravagantly lashed eyes fixed on her face, he rubbed a finger hard across the bridge of his nose; the gesture was one of intense weariness.

Lucy looked at him and saw what anger and fear had prevented her from seeing up until now. The over-bright glitter in his spectacular eyes suggested he had gone a long time without sleep. The dark smudges beneath those deep-set eyes and the lines deeply etched in the area between his mouth and aquiline nose accented her initial conclusion.

There was absolutely no reason for her to care if he drove himself into an early grave by making unreasonable demands on his body, which would of course be totally typical of the man. There were far more deserving and worthy causes for her anxiety and concern.

'Oh, I know you'd not go to that much trouble just to get me into bed.'

Finn stopped dead in the process of running a hand across his unshaven jaw. He might be tired but the eyes that skimmed across her face felt uncomfortably keen to Lucy.

'Still promoting yourself as zealously as ever, I see.' The wry flick of anger in his eyes made her shift uncomfortably. 'Actually, what I was about to explain was that I won't be there very much, if at all.'

'Why me?' she asked bluntly.

Finn made a dismissive sound in his throat. 'I've told you...'

'No, actually, you haven't. There must be agencies that could provide you with a nanny a lot better qualified than me.'

'Some people might think I owe you a job?'

'But not you.'

'No,' he agreed, 'not me.'

Lucy was wondering why he was being so evasive when an unacceptable possibility occurred to her. '*Oh, no!*' she gasped.

'Oh, no, what?'

'Annie didn't...she didn't ask you to do this, did she?'

she queried suspiciously. 'You didn't invent a job for me because she asked you to, because you feel guilty?'

'You think I arranged for Alice to slip on the building block and break her arm…?'

His amused look made Lucy feel like a raving lunatic for coming up with the wild idea.

'Alice is Liam's nanny?'

'You really weren't listening to me, were you?' Finn observed, not appearing to notice her discomfiture. 'We are talking *serious* bad timing here, Lucy,' he explained, no longer looking amused as he contemplated his childcare situation. '*Normally* my schedule is flexible.'

'But not now?'

He shook his head. 'No, not now,' he agreed. 'And I can't leave just anyone in charge of Liam.'

'Agencies vet people.'

'I've no intention of taking an agency's word for the character of someone who will have sole care of the most precious thing I possess. Where Liam is concerned,' he explained, 'I err on the side of caution. I do my own screening and that takes time…I don't have time. I suppose you're wondering about the money.'

'No.' She could almost see Annie groaning; *know your worth* was one of her sister's favourite sayings.

He mentioned a sum which made her eyes widen and would have impressed even Annie—now, that would solve quite a few problems. But at what price?

Her unfocused thoughts kept returning to what he had said…she wasn't *just anyone*, information which quite irrationally gave her a warm glow of well-being, but this didn't tell Lucy what she was to him. You're not anything to him except convenient, Lucy, the cold voice of self-preservation reminded her—between the sheets and outside them.

'You haven't screened me,' she protested feebly. Her eyes widened. *'Have you?'* Maybe his screening process involved sleeping with his prospective employees…?

'I don't need to.' He didn't offer any explanation as to why she was the exception to the rule and Lucy was too busy wondering why this preposterous idea was sounding more attractive with each passing second.

'You're saying you'd trust me with your son?' Of course, the money was a lot more than a supermarket job and it would be extraordinarily useful.

'Are you saying you'll take the job?' he countered.

She couldn't…*could she*…?

'I…I…'

'Of course, I can see you're quite comfortable here…' he remarked with a casual glance around the tastefully furnished room.

Lucy coloured. 'This is only a temporary measure,' she grunted with a frown.

'Your sister seems more than happy to have you stay as long as you need.'

Lucy's lips pursed. 'I am not going to sponge off my sister!'

'Fine,' he smiled, 'then take this job and reassert your independence.'

He was shameless! Such blatantly manipulative, sneaky tactics made her want to hit him. 'You must see that it would be impossible for me to work for you?'

Her appeal fell on deaf ears. 'Why?'

'Because…' Her lips puckered in frustration. It was true—what legitimate reason did she have for refusing a perfectly good, indecently paid job? Except that she had the promise of another one—less well paid maybe but one that wouldn't bring her into contact with Finn Fitzgerald.

Was that why she hadn't mentioned the other job, so that

he'd carry on thinking her choice was one of necessity not desire? Could it be that some masochistic part of her wanted this?

'It would be disloyal…to Annie.'

'Well, Annie didn't seem to think so. She was actually very enthusiastic. She seemed to think it would be good for you,' Finn recalled thoughtfully.

Lucy stared at him, transfixed. 'You discussed it with my sister?' With each successive syllable her voice rose in volume and pitch until she arrived, breathless, at a gentle shriek.

'I know I ought to have asked you first…but we got talking…your sister is a very easy woman to talk to,' he observed thoughtfully.

Lucy gave a sickly grin. 'Yes, she got the double dose of empathy in the family, but she missed out on the suspicion altogether,' she responded with heavy irony that brought a gleam of amusement to his eyes. '*She* takes people at face value.'

It was pretty obvious to Lucy that Finn had had her sister eating out of his hand. She tried very hard not to think about other personal details her garrulous sibling might have seen fit to share with this man.

'In future, if you want to know something about me, come and ask me, don't go behind my back.'

Their eyes meshed. The heavy silence between them stretched until Finn sighed.

'If your sister doesn't hold me to blame for their split-up, Lucy, why should you…?'

'I think she might if I told her you slept with me to find out where she and Connor were staying.'

He didn't even have the decency to look embarrassed.

'I wondered about that…' he admitted. 'You didn't tell her, then?'

'It's hardly the sort of thing I'm going to boast about.'

Finn felt a swell of anger, which some sane, objective portion of his brain was conscious of being totally out of proportion with the taunt. What the hell was happening to him?

'Besides,' Lucy continued through clenched teeth, 'she was miserable enough without listening to me moaning about my disastrous one-night stand.'

'I wouldn't call it disastrous.'

'Well, I would.'

'And,' he added, frowning, 'it wasn't a one-night stand. I don't do one—night stands,' he announced, looking deeply affronted.

'Oh, and you think I do!' she bellowed back.

'Not according to your sister,' he admitted casually.

Lucy froze. 'Annie discussed my sex life with you?' Annie was dead.

'Not as such, although I did get the impression she was glad Rupert was out of your life, but was worried he might have put you off men permanently.'

'And I suppose you told her otherwise...' She closed her eyes and shook her head. 'God, I wish I was an only child!' she groaned.

'How many men were there in between Rupert and me? A ball-park figure...round it up to the nearest ten.'

This was just too much for Lucy. 'A hundred!' she yelled. 'But don't worry, you measured up pretty well. Does this sort of thing turn you on or something?' she demanded scornfully. 'I just don't believe any of this, and Annie is a fine one to be talking about the state of anyone's sex life when she...' She suddenly stopped dead.

'She?'

Lucy shook her head, appalled at what her anger had almost made her reveal.

The indentation between his dark brows deepened as Finn watched her squirm uncomfortably. 'My God!' An expression of almost comical shock washed over his face. 'You were about to say she's a virgin, weren't you?'

'Well, there's no law against it, is there?' Lucy growled belligerently.

Annie with one lover to her name and me with two—it made you wonder if this was all about genes. It would seem the Foster women just had low sex drives. Though when she looked at Finn it didn't feel that way. When she looked at Finn rampant and out of control were more accurate terms to describe the way she felt.

A low laugh was torn from Finn's throat, but he still looked shaken. 'It's just a bit unusual,' he observed mildly.

'There are a lot more around than you think, and anyway she's no longer an *oddity*—your precious brother saw to that.'

'Do you suppose he knew?'

'Why don't you ask him the next time you compare notes—how the hell should I know if he knew?' she yelled. 'Do you mind if we change the subject and, incidentally, if you tell Annie I told you there will be no place to hide.'

'I can understand your reluctance to get involved with someone after the Rupert fiasco.'

'Who said it was a fiasco?'

'Annie.'

If Annie hadn't been suffering enough to satisfy the most vindictive of individuals Lucy would have arranged it so that she did.

'And as far as definitions go,' she added, reminded of a point she still had to make, 'sleeping with someone, often a total stranger with whom you have nothing in common and don't even like on a one-off, never-to-be-repeated basis, frequently regretted the next day is definitely a one-night stand! Is any of this sounding familiar to you?'

A slow, dangerous smile spread across his clean-cut features as he met her scornful glare head-on. 'How can you be so sure it's not going to be repeated?'

Lucy went hot and cold, then hot all over again. Then, making a superhuman effort to pull herself together, she closed her mouth with a snap and lifted her chin.

'I'm *extremely* sure,' she replied in a high, shaky voice.

Finn didn't call her a liar but he didn't need to—his expression said it all.

'You should have more faith…' he responded in a raspy voice that sent shivers up her spine. 'And an open mind, then you wouldn't close yourself off from all sorts of interesting possibilities.'

'I have a very open mind and I'm not interested in the sort of possibilities you're talking about.' She might convince him but there was no way her body was falling for that one. Her skin was prickling with heat.

'Sure you are.'

He was looking at the outline of her brazenly erect nipples. At least he'd stopped pretending he was any sort of gentleman; if she had had control of her limbs Lucy would have smacked him.

His long lashes lifted off his carved cheekbones. The hot blue of his eyes literally dazzled her. 'And so am I.'

Lucy had literally no control over the soft hiss of lust that emerged from her parted lips.

'I think we have to be realistic here,' he suggested in a low, intense voice.

He could speak for himself; Lucy had no wish to be realistic, not when that realism involved facing up to several unpalatable realities—like where Finn was concerned she was everything she despised most in her own sex...a total spineless pushover!

'You can't ignore this sort of sexual chemistry and expect it to go away. Just because our respective siblings have messed up...'

'Respective nothing, your brother did the messing up, my sister got messed.'

'I don't disagree with you.'

'You don't?' she echoed incredulously.

'No. Now, will you shut up so that I can say what I've been trying to?'

Lucy opened her mouth to complain about being spoken to this way and then saw the way he was looking at her and closed it again. With the skin drawn tight over his tense, hard-boned features and his eyes narrowed Finn looked like a man perilously close to losing control. Though some reckless part of her wanted to supply that final push and see what happened. It was the cautious Lucy that, after a short internal struggle, won the day on this occasion.

'*Thank you,*' he drawled with sarcastic emphasis when she subsided. 'I was trying to say that I don't see why their history should preclude us from continuing to see one another.'

'I don't date.' This entire conversation had a pronounced sense of unreality about it.

'After Rupert I'm not surprised, but actually neither do I.'

'You don't what?'

'Date,' he elaborated with a grimace.

'Then what are you suggesting? We just have sex...' Her laugh tailed off as she met his eyes. 'God, that is what you're saying, isn't it?' she gasped.

'I seem to remember you telling me almost as soon as we met that sex was a great way to relax after a bad day.'

'*You* are the cause of all my bad days, all my headaches and all my sleepless nights...' she retorted indiscreetly. 'And it's also sort of relevant that I wouldn't trust you as far as I could throw you. You used me.'

'Maybe I did but only to the same extent you used me.' His sardonic look of enquiry made her grit her teeth.

'I didn't use you!'

'It wasn't a complaint,' he soothed, smiling into her angry face. 'As far as I'm concerned you can use me any time you like.'

'Don't hold your breath,' she muttered as the feeling low in her belly became physically painful.

'It was just a thought.'

And one not important enough for him to push apparently.

'I know it looks bad, but I did not have any ulterior motive for spending the night with you, Lucy. I wasn't lying awake waiting for you to talk in your sleep.' No, he'd been lying awake because looking at her sleeping face had seemed a better use of his time than sleeping.

'But when the opportunity arose you took it.'

He made no attempt to deny her bitter accusation. 'And I can't honestly say I'd do it differently if I had the call to make again. My own nights haven't been so peaceful of late if that's any comfort,' he added wryly. 'But let's put aside our personal feelings for the moment...'

Lucy stared; he said it as if it was possible! Maybe it was for him, maybe he could turn his feelings on and off, but she couldn't.

'You need a job, and Liam needs a nanny. Pride is fine but it doesn't pay the bills.'

A job in a supermarket would though, and it wouldn't bring her into contact with Finn Fitzgerald.

'If I say yes…' She lifted her head and caught the tail end of a look of smug satisfaction on his face. 'Hypothetically speaking,' she gritted.

'Of course.'

'What would I be saying yes to?'

'Flying with me to Dublin tomorrow morning to meet Liam. You could get to know one another on the drive down to the beach house.'

'Who is looking after him at the moment?'

'Bridie…she keeps house for Dad and looked after Con when he was growing up. She'll come with you to the beach house; she used to when Con and I were kids. You wouldn't have to worry about meals and so forth; she'd take care of that side of things.'

'It doesn't sound to me as though you need a nanny.'

'Bridie adores Liam,' he agreed, 'and she's more than capable, but she's not getting any younger and Liam is pretty lively. I'm just worried she would exhaust herself trying to keep up with him.'

'And you will be…?'

'What's wrong, Lucy, don't you trust yourself?'

Lucy's head came up with an indignant snap. The amusement faded from his face as their glances locked. What replaced it sent her heart slamming hard against her ribcage.

'It's not *me* I'm worried about,' she retorted thickly.

'Why don't you tell me what you are worried about, Lucy…?' he encouraged in a soft, dangerous voice.

'Well, as you've asked, I'm worried about you getting the idea that paying my salary gives you entry to my bed.'

His expression remained as enigmatic as ever, but Lucy

found herself thinking that maybe she could have phrased it a little more tactfully.

'I think it's best to get these things out in the open so there are no misunderstandings...' She faltered suddenly, thinking maybe it hadn't been such a good idea to share her concerns.

'Just for the record, Lucy, I've never had to pay for it.'

Lucy blushed deeply at the deliberate crudity.

'And if you're asking me to make some sort of written guarantee...' He shook his head. 'I'm not the one with the problem distinguishing my personal life from business, neither do I have a problem admitting that I want you...I've absolutely no intention of offering you empty promises. I'm not going to say I won't make love to you because for the past few days I haven't been able to think about much else.'

'I don't believe you.' But she wanted to...how she wanted to.

'I understand that I hurt you when I left.'

'It was no big deal.'

Her careless shrug said one thing but the hurt in her wide eyes said something else.

'It was a big deal,' he disagreed. 'I don't want to hurt you, Lucy. It's the last thing I want to do.'

'You can't be hurt by someone unless you care about them and I don't care about you, Finn,' she flung coldly.

Before his dark lashes swept downwards in a concealing curtain Lucy thought she saw something extraordinary written on his drawn features—pain, and for a split-second she wanted to retract her words.

The compulsion to offer comfort vanished when Finn responded with an expression that conveyed such total indifference to her comments that she knew she had been mistaken.

'Well, that might work out best all round in the long

run,' he mused with an offhand shrug. 'The flight is at ten-thirty; I'll send a car for you at nine. Is there anything you want to ask me?'

It was only after he'd gone that she realised she had never actually said yes.

CHAPTER ELEVEN

THE following morning Annie insisted that Lucy open her already packed suitcase to put in a dress. Since Lucy had told her about the job the previous evening Annie had almost seemed her old bubbly self. She might be thinking she had made the worst call of her life but it was almost worth it just to see some animation on her sister's pale face.

'You never know when you might need it,' Annie explained to her less worldly-wise sister as she laid the essential item on top of the more practical clothing Lucy had packed the previous night.

'If you say so, Annie.'

'I know you don't like Finn,' Annie remarked in a tone that suggested she found this circumstance totally inexplicable. 'But I'm really glad you said yes, Lucy. I mean, it's not much fun for you hanging around here.'

'And the money is good.'

'Oh, I hope you're not doing it just because of that.'

Annie looked so distressed by the idea that Lucy hastened to assure her that this was not the case. She did such a good job of selling the job to Annie that she almost convinced herself her stomach didn't knot in anxiety every time she thought of what she had committed herself to.

'I know you're used to looking after yourself, but I'll feel so much better knowing that you're in a safe pair of hands,' Annie admitted as Lucy replaced the lid on the suitcase. 'Are you all right?' she added anxiously as her sister began to choke.

'Fine,' Lucy promised hoarsely as she massaged her neck

nervously. *Safe hands?* Are we both talking about the same person?

When Lucy looked at Finn's hands she didn't think *safe* or *secure*!

A shatteringly erotic image of his large brown hand curved over her pale breast, his thumb moving confidently over the swollen nub at its centre, flashed across her vision. The retrieved memory was so powerful it blocked out everything else. It was the sound of the key which had fallen from her nerveless fingers landing on the polished boards that finally jolted her back to the present.

'And I don't have to worry about you because I know he'll look after you,' Annie added happily as Lucy scrabbled on the floor to retrieve her key. 'Here, let me,' she added, sitting on top of the case as Lucy began to struggle silently to close it.

'I hope you packed plenty of waterproofs—Ireland's the greenest place on earth for a good reason,' she added, oblivious to the effect her casual comment had had on her sister. If she had thought about it, which she didn't, she would have put Lucy's raised colour down to the struggle she was having to close the suitcase. 'It rains. I know someone who went to Ireland last year and it rained for the whole week.'

'Cheer me up, why don't you? Annie...' The lock finally clicked and Lucy took up a cross-legged posture on the bed. A horrid thought had occurred to her. 'I don't suppose you asked him to, did you? When you took that phone message.'

'Asked who what?'

'Asked Finn to...to look after me.'

'I might have said something like that, and why shouldn't I?' Annie responded defensively.

'Oh, God!' Lucy groaned, rocking forward, her head in her hands.

'I don't know why you're being like this,' Annie observed indignantly. 'He didn't mind at all.'

I just bet he didn't. She was tempted to tell her helpful sibling just what sort of looking after Finn probably had in mind.

'You're going to ruin your hair doing that,' Annie observed as Lucy stuffed a pillow on top of her head. 'See, I told you so,' she said when Lucy emerged in a tousled condition.

'What makes you think I need looking after? I'm not a child, Annie. He's my boss, not my damned uncle. It's embarrassing.'

She glared at her sister and saw with dismay the glistening tears standing out in her sister's eyes begin to silently overflow down her cheeks.

'I…I'm sorry,' Annie sniffed, 'I meant it for the best. I worry about you…'

'Oh, Annie!' Lucy exclaimed. 'It's fine, really it is. I didn't mean to upset you, I don't mind…' She slipped off the bed and placed her arms around her sobbing sister. 'I'm not sure I feel right about leaving you just now.'

'Oh, don't be silly, Luce.' Annie gave a watery but cheerful smile. 'I don't know why I'm crying; just lately I can't seem to stop.'

Lucy's tender heart ached. 'You'll meet someone else.'

Her sister drew a shuddering sigh and drew back. 'I don't think I want to,' she observed bleakly before turning briskly back to the task in hand. 'Now, have you got any shoes in there to go with that dress?'

Finn was seated three rows back from her on the short flight over from Heathrow and she was seated next to a young man who immediately announced he was nervous about flying. He went on to explain that when he was nervous he talked—he wasn't lying.

By the time they touched down Lucy knew his life history including a lot of personal details she could have done without knowing! Before they disembarked he warmly thanked her and insisted on giving her his address with instructions that she should drop in if she was ever down that way.

'This might sound stupid but I just feel so close to you,' he said, taking her hand and pressing it between his.

'Sorry to interrupt,' Finn, sounding anything but, drawled. 'Are you ready, Lucy? We have a schedule...'

For someone with a natural presence he had a worrying ability to creep up on a person.

Despite Finn's dark, disapproving presence hanging over them, Lucy returned the pressure of her companion's fingers before sliding the strap of her tote bag over her shoulder.

'I was just coming.'

Finn, his eyes cold as flint, nodded briefly at the other man before walking away.

Lucy felt as if she had to compensate for Finn's lack of manners. 'He's my boss.' And keen to remind her of that, it would seem, if that display was any indication! If this was the way things were going to be the sooner the better he left for whatever high-powered meeting he'd been preparing for.

'I hope I didn't get you in trouble,' her new friend said. 'He didn't look very happy,' he observed with a doubtful look at the back of the tall retreating figure.

'I expect he didn't get as much work done on the flight as he wanted to. Don't worry, I can handle Finn,' she announced in the vain hope that this was true.

Lucy, feeling very much like the luggage, but less welcome, tagged along behind Finn, who seemed to be in a foul humour. Whatever it was he had on his mind he was obviously in no mood to make small talk. In fact he didn't say a word to her until after he'd stowed the luggage in the boot of a silver-coloured Jag.

'A friend of yours?'

The abrupt question took her unawares. *'Who?'*

His jaw tightened as he came around to open the door for her. 'The guy you were holding hands with.'

'Oh, that was Charlie.'

'Charlie who?'

She frowned. 'Does it matter?' His persistence puzzled her.

'Matter!' Finn studied her face, his expression one of austere distaste. 'Yes, I think it does actually if you intend to go around recklessly picking up any strange man who takes your fancy when you're in charge of my son.'

This extraordinary and extremely unfair accusation took her breath away. *Pick up strange men?* She had not the faintest idea what he was talking about.

'I presumed that I didn't have to say this to you, but after your inappropriate conduct today it might be better if I spell it out. I expect any personal details I might have discussed with you pertaining to Liam do not go any further.'

She angled her chin so that she could see his face more clearly; there was a shaft of light from a skylight falling directly into her eyes and she recoiled with a gasp away from the furious contempt she saw there.

'Do you want me to sign something?'

'That won't be necessary.'

'I was being ironic.'

'I wasn't. Continuity is important to children.'

His harsh observation brought Annie's description of his own childhood to mind.

'Which is why he doesn't have a constant stream of *aunties* in his life.'

'Your lovers?'

'Exactly.'

'What *exactly* are you asking me to do, Finn?'

'I'm asking you to be…circumspect about our relationship.'

'You think I'm going to tell your eight-year-old son I slept with you?' Her voice dropped to an incredulous whisper. 'You think I'm going to tell anyone? Why are you behaving this way, Finn?' she asked him quietly, too confused by his irrational hostility to be feel angered by the appalling way he was treating her.

'Why?' he ejaculated, his chest swelling with the sense of outrage that consumed him. 'You were talking to him continually for the entire trip!' he recalled, running a hand roughly along his jaw.

It took her several seconds to realise what he was talking about. When it clicked her mouth fell open. Did that mean he'd been looking at her for the entire journey?

'I thought you were going to work on the flight, not spy on me.'

'How was I meant to work while my travelling companion…my *lover*, was making a spectacle of herself?'

'I came here in the capacity of nanny, not your mistress.'

The interruption appeared to incense him further. 'I don't like to think how far your *friendship* with that *hippy* would have progressed had we been on a long-haul flight.'

A little thrill of neat electricity had run through her body when he'd said 'lover'. If she hadn't been so distracted she might have fitted the final piece of the jigsaw a little faster.

But finally it did hit her and the idea was so incredible she laughed out loud.

'My God, you're jealous!'

'*Jealous,*' he said with a derisive laugh. 'That is totally…' Halfway through delivering a forceful denial she saw an awareness flicker at the backs of his eyes. 'I've never been jealous of a woman in my life.'

'The man was scared of flying; he talked to me to distract himself,' she explained quietly.

Finn exhaled loudly and, elbow braced against the roof of the car, he pressed his forehead into the heel of his hand. His dark hair flopped across his forehead, concealing his expression from her, but she could see the wash of colour that ran up under his smooth, olive-toned skin.

When he straightened up he scrubbed both hands roughly over his face like someone who was trying to wake themselves up.

'Get in the car,' he said abruptly without looking at her. Then added in a goaded tone just before he closed the door, 'You're so naïve. That *I'm afraid of flying line* is probably a tried and tested chat-up line.'

'I think I can tell the difference between a chat-up line and genuine fear.' The door slammed before she had finished speaking.

During the short journey to his home the word 'jealousy' was not mentioned but it was there, a silent presence hanging in the air between them.

The house almost exactly mirrored her mental image of a perfect family home. A large, solid building of Edwardian origin set at the end of a tree-lined drive, inside which the furnishings were a comfortable mixture of modern and traditional.

As soon as they stepped into the hallway a small figure flung himself at Finn like a heat-seeking missile. The expression on Finn's face as he hugged his son brought an emotional lump to Lucy's throat. As she listened to the teasing exchange it was clear to Lucy that father and son had a very close relationship.

'You'll have the boy throwing up—he's only just had his lunch,' observed a small figure who had been watching the reunion with an indulgent smile.

'Hello, Bridie, how are you?'

'I'm grand, thank you. Where are your manners, Liam? Say hello to the lady.'

'This is, Lucy; she'll be looking after you until Alice's arm is better,' Finn said, taking his son by the hand and drawing him towards her. 'This is my son, Liam.'

Considering the heartbreaking likeness between father and son, the introduction was unnecessary.

'Hello, Liam,' Lucy said, smiling.

'How about if you show Lucy the garden, Liam,' his father suggested. His son nodded eagerly but Bridie intervened, her manner regretful.

'That would be nice, but Liam is off to Patrick's for tea…the Kennedys are picking him up any minute now. It's been arranged for an age,' Bridie added quickly when Finn frowned.

'Perhaps when you come back, Liam…?' Lucy suggested, smiling.

The boy looked to Bridie for guidance.

'I'm afraid it will be dark by then, Miss Foster.' Bridie took the boy by the shoulders with a recommendation to, 'Go look out for Mrs Kennedy,' and turned to Lucy. 'I expect you'd like to see your room, miss.'

'Lucy, please.'

The grey-haired woman gave a noncommittal nod; her sharp hazel eyes remained cold.

'I'll show Lucy up…have you put her in the one next to—?' Finn began.

'I'm just in the middle of giving that room a spring clean, and don't you be worrying yourself—I'll see the young lady up.' When Finn showed signs of objecting she explained there were several urgent phone messages awaiting his scrutiny in his study.

All this was done with a smile but Lucy was left with the distinct impression that Bridie was going to make it her business to ensure Lucy saw as little of the Fitzgerald males—senior and junior—as possible.

She actually felt a good deal of sympathy for the older woman, who obviously didn't like the idea of an unknown younger woman muscling in on her territory.

'This is a lovely room,' she said when Bridie opened a door to a small but prettily decorated room.

'It's north-facing, so it doesn't get the sun.'

'What pretty flowers.'

There was still no thawing in the other woman's manner towards her. 'The boy put them there,' she revealed unsmilingly. 'He's a lovely child and no trouble at all. I'm sure I don't know what you'll do with yourself.'

'I expect Finn thought I could take some of the pressure off you.'

The small woman drew herself up to her full height. 'I'm not quite in my dotage yet.'

Lucy looked dismayed. 'No, of course not; I didn't mean—'

'Dinner's at seven,' Bridie interrupted abruptly. 'I'll have your things brought up.'

'Oh, let me; Finn is busy.'

'*Mr* Fitzgerald,' the other woman replied, emphasising his title, 'won't be bothering himself,' she promised. 'It's Joseph's day for the garden; I'll get him to fetch them up.'

The door closed and Lucy sat down on the bed, a dejected slump to her shoulders.

Could this be going any worse?

She barely had time to reflect on the total awfulness of the situation when there was a knock on the door.

She got up and smoothed down her hair. The way things were going it seemed inevitable that Joseph, whose day it was for the garden, would take an instant dislike to her too.

'Come in,' she called cheerfully. 'Finn...!' she gasped as his tall figure was framed in the doorway.

'I don't know why the hell Bridie put you in here—it's the smallest room in the house,' he complained, looking around the neat room with a dissatisfied frown.

Lucy didn't explain that that was probably exactly why she had put her there and if it was also the most distant from the master bedroom that had probably been an added bonus!

'It's fine, Finn.' She nervously wiped her sweaty palms down her denim-covered thighs. 'Thank you for bringing them up.' Please let him go before I do something really stupid.

He placed the bags on the floor. 'I'll get her to move you,' he announced.

'God, no, don't do that!' she cried in some alarm. That would really make Bridie warm to her. 'It's only for one night and I *like* it,' she added firmly.

Finn shrugged. 'As you wish.'

She waited, but he didn't move.

'I can't come with you tomorrow,' he finally announced abruptly. 'You'll have to drive down. I'll leave you a route map.'

'You want me to drive...?' Heavens, he wasn't expecting her to drive that enormous Jag of his, was he...? 'Not your car? The Jaguar…?' She shuddered at the thought of that gleaming monster.

'The luggage won't fit in the hatchback. You'll be fine,' he added, dismissing her concern with a casual wave of his hand. 'Bridie will navigate for you.'

Lucy gave a strained smile. 'What if I scratch it?'

'It's not a hanging offence,' he observed, sounding amused but strained.

It occurred to her that all the time Finn had been in the room he had looked just about everywhere but at her.

She was miserably thinking that he couldn't stand the sight of her when his smoky blue eyes finally found their way to hers. The intensity of his stare and the conflict it contained shocked her deeply.

'Is something wrong, Finn?'

'Yes.'

His brooding contemplation did not lessen as the silence between them once more stretched.

'Do you want…?'

'Don't say anything.' He took a deep breath and dragged a hand through his sleek dark hair. 'Not until you've heard what I've got to say…'

Unable to imagine what he could possibly want to tell her that could account for his abrupt and peculiar manner, Lucy nodded.

'You were right, I was jealous…'

Lucy drew a startled breath—this was the very last thing she had expected to hear.

'I acted like a total idiot because I was jealous of you talking to another man when *I* wanted to talk to you…I wanted to hear you laugh…I wanted you to touch my arm,' he divulged aggressively.

Lucy swallowed to lubricate her bone-dry throat; her

heart was banging so loudly she could barely hear herself think, not that she was capable at that point of thinking.

'I know we've not had the best of starts.' Finn revealed his teeth in a savagely self-derisive smile. The dark colour ran across the chiselled angle of his cheekbones, bringing them into prominence. 'I'd like to...*date* you.'

'*Date?*' she parroted. 'You don't date.'

'Neither, as I recall, do you,' he cut back. 'Listen, if you're going to throw every stupid thing I've said in my face I'll be late for my flight.' There was urgency as well as wry humour in his expression as he gazed down into her upturned face. The humour abruptly faded as his eyes moved over the soft contours of her face. 'I want you in my bed, but that's not enough...it's always been enough before, but you're different. I'm trying to say—really badly—that I want you in my life...I *need* you in my life.' As he waited for her response, she could almost feel the waves of raw frustration emanating from him. 'Good God, woman,' he grated hoarsely, when he was unable to contain himself any longer, 'will you say something?'

A sudden brilliant smile illuminated her shocked face. 'Yes, please!' she cried as she launched herself into his arms.

Finn caught her softly supple body to him, almost driving the air from her lungs with an embrace that lifted her feet from the ground. She felt him shudder hard against her before his lips covered her own. With a moan Lucy opened her mouth to the intimate stabbing invasion of his tongue and wound her arms around his neck.

When his head lifted they were both panting. Lucy looked at his incredibly handsome face, flushed at the moment with passion, and released a laugh of sheer delight.

'What's so funny...?' he asked, stroking the side of her

face. His finger left tingly trails across her slightly damp skin.

'Bridie is not going to approve of this.'

'Why wouldn't she?'

'She doesn't like me,' Lucy explained, flicking her tongue experimentally over the palm of his hand where it lay lightly against the side of her face.

Finn sucked in his breath and his eyes darkened dramatically as he felt the flick of her tongue over his skin.

His skin was salty…she liked it; she liked even better the pulsing surge of his erection as it ground into her belly.

She slanted him a sultry look from under her lashes. 'You taste good. Do you taste that good all over…?'

Finn groaned and caught the hand that was delicately slipping the buttons on his shirt. 'Lucy, don't!'

Lucy pouted. 'You don't like it?' It had felt to her as though he did—quite a lot.

'I like it very much,' he grated hoarsely, 'as you well know, but I've got a flight to catch.'

'Do you have to go…?'

'Do you think I'd be leaving if there was any alternative?' he asked her, looking very much like a man in agony.

With an apologetic smile Lucy backed away. 'Sorry, it's just I've been thinking about touching you for so long…' She saw the expression on his face and stopped. 'That's not helping, is it?' The feeling of being irresistible was actually one she might be able to get used to.

'Not exactly,' he confirmed drily. 'I really *do* have to go…' He looked at his watch and clicked his tongue in irritation.

Lucy nodded unhappily. She reached up and pressed a chaste kiss to his lean cheek. 'Bye, Finn.'

He looked down at her with a dangerous glitter in his sapphire-blue eyes. 'You call that goodbye…?'

'I was being considerate.'

'To hell with considerate!' he declared, bending his head to place a kiss on her lips that could by no stretch of the imagination be considered chaste!

Lucy staggered back, a dazed expression in her eyes, when he finally released her.

'Something to think about while I'm gone.'

CHAPTER TWELVE

FINN had rung every day during the week he'd been away, but Lucy felt inhibited talking to him on the phone; the things she said came out wrong or sounded forced and awkward. She needed to see his face when she told him how she felt. Finn had no such inhibitions; the previous night he had told her that when he thought of her it was always on a beach.

'When I come home I'm going to make love to you on the beach.'

'But what if people see us?'

His rich, wicked laughter rang out at her shocked reply.

'They'll be jealous,' he told her, sounding almost as if he liked the idea of it happening.

'I'm beginning to think you are a warped and twisted person.'

'When I come back I'll show you just how warped,' he promised throatily.

'How will you do that?' she whispered.

He told her—in detail.

The frustration of being apart was worse than anything Lucy had ever experienced, and now she knew he was coming back the anticipation of his return the following day was almost as stressful.

The Bridie situation hadn't helped. Her first instincts had been correct. The older woman deeply resented her presence and disapproved of the growing friendship developing between Lucy and the young boy.

Lucy's expression lightened as she thought of him. Liam

161

was a delight; a bright, affectionate child with a remarkably even temperament who could on occasion be incredibly stubborn.

Lucy had seen a demonstration of his stubbornness their first day there. Alerted by the sounds of loud voices, she had discovered Liam in the bottom of the garden beside the footpath that led to the beach.

He'd had his arms around an ugly-looking mongrel and was yelling at a group of jeering teenagers.

'They were kicking him, Lucy!' he cried when he saw her.

'He's ours—we can do what we like with him,' the ringleader announced sullenly.

'And it's useless,' another added to the sound of general laughter.

'You're not having him,' Liam declared, his small face red with outrage. 'I shan't let them, Lucy.'

'Go and take the dog back to the house, Liam,' she said quietly. The child shot her a look of gratitude that brought a lump to her throat.

The gang's protests quietened quickly enough when Lucy, who judged it useless to appeal to their humanity, offered them money. They haggled for more but it didn't take long for an understanding to be reached that pleased all parties…

Except Bridie!

She pronounced the animal to be ugly, a claim Lucy couldn't deny, and a health hazard that was probably not house-broken. After checking that the dog didn't have an owner Lucy promised to be personally responsible for any damage the animal did, clean up any mess and make sure he was a flea-free zone, but it was Liam's appeals that had swung it.

In private Bridie had told Lucy that she had exceeded

her authority by allowing a dangerous animal into the house and she had every intention of bringing the matter to Finn's attention the moment he got home.

The *dangerous animal* came with them that morning to the beach. After three days of solid rain, like any little boy who'd been cooped up for that long, Liam was bursting to get outdoors. Despite Bridie's objections that it was far too cold, they took a picnic lunch which they set down in the sand dunes with a rug, before walking down to the beach.

The great swathe of almost white sand was totally empty and breathtaking set against a clear blue sky. Liam with the dog at his heels spent a long time making his mark in the smooth, virgin sand.

Lucy wisely let him run off some excess energy. After a while he tired of the game and returned to where she was watching.

'Can we collect shells now?'

'Sure thing.' Liam's collection now filled just about every window sill in the house.

'I told Dad last night you let me have a dog.'

Oh, God…!

'And what did he say?'

'He said he'd have to thank you for it when he sees you,' Liam replied cheerfully.

'Lucy…?'

'Yes?'

Liam shuffled his bottom onto a rock covered in green slime and lifted his face to hers. 'Do you have a mum?'

Lucy's heart ached as she saw where this was going. 'Yes, I do.'

'So do I, only she's not a real mum, one that lives with us. I'd quite like a real mum,' he explained, raising soulful eyes that would have melted the ice cap let alone her soft heart.

'Well, you've got a very nice dad.'

The waif-in-the-storm expression vanished, leaving on the soft, childish features a look of strong resolution. The resemblance to his father was so marked Lucy caught her breath.

'You like him, then.' He gave a small sigh of satisfaction. 'I thought you did.'

This from an eight-year-old…my indifference needs some serious work.

'Your father is a…nice man,' she finished lamely.

'If you married him you could be my mum…I could do with a female influence in my life.'

Lucy was taken aback by this solemn pronouncement. 'Is that so?'

Liam nodded. 'Dad's worried about that. I heard him and Uncle Con talking about it. Dad probably needs a female influence too.'

Lucy shook her head. 'It's a nice idea, Liam, but grown-ups only get married when they love one another very much.'

His little face dropped. 'You could make him love you.'

Lucy swallowed the lump in her throat. 'You can't make people love you, sweetheart.' But she was going to give it her best shot.

'You'd be a good mum—you don't get cross when I get dirty and you know quite a lot about football, for a girl.' Leaving it at that, he ran off with the dog at his heels.

Lucy allowed him to go before she allowed her feelings to show. With a groan of *Why do these things happen to me…?* she flopped back on the sand and stared at the clouds scudding across the blue sky.

All she needed was Finn to get the idea she'd been putting ideas into the boy's head. She could imagine what his reaction would be if he thought she had used Liam in a cynical attempt to get a ring on her finger.

She was still lying there when the dog returned and licked her face affectionately.

'Yuck!' she cried, leaping to her feet. The dog wagged his tail happily and Liam giggled to see her wipe her face.

When they got back to the house the place was filled with pleasant smells; whatever else Bridie was, she was a very good cook. Liam ran off to the kitchen in search of cookies and Lucy headed for her room. She was halfway up the stairs when Bridie called her.

'A person who said she was your sister rang when you were out, miss.'

Lucy resisted asking why anyone would say they were her sister unless they were. 'Did she leave a message?'

'She asked would you call her back...she seemed a bit upset.'

Lucy came down the stairs two at a time. 'How long ago did she ring?' she asked as she dialled.

'About ten-thirty, I'd say.'

Lucy glanced at her watch; almost an hour and a half ago. As she waited for Annie to pick up she told herself there was no point being alarmed; it might be nothing, she told herself.

It was something, though it was impossible from the limited information Annie gave her to know what exactly. Every time she asked her sister if she was ill Annie said no and started crying all over again. The only thing she was clear about was that she needed her sister back home right away.

She had a lucky break when she managed to get a cancellation on the next flight later that day.

'I don't want you to go,' Liam said when she was about to leave.

Lucy saw he was fighting back tears, which made her own eyes fill. Blinking them back, she hunkered down to his level and held out her arms.

'Come give me a hug.' Liam walked right into her arms and gave her a kiss on the cheek. Lucy brushed a dark curl lovingly off his face. 'I don't want to go either, love, but I have to and your daddy will be home in the morning.'

The little boy looked a little more cheerful when she reminded him of this.

'I might need my dog to sleep on my bed tonight...' he said, looking at Bridie.

'Just this once,' she said sternly. 'Now, off you go indoors.'

'Thank you,' Lucy said as the other woman passed one of her bags into the taxi. 'You will explain to Mr Fitzgerald that there was a family emergency, won't you...?'

'Don't you worry your head, I'll see to everything,' Bridie promised.

After not hearing from Finn for weeks, Lucy finally got hold of him, only for him to calmly tell that he wanted her out of his life. But now Lucy had to confront him for her sister's sake. Lucy had chosen her outfit with care. She wanted to look like the sort of person airlines offered upgrades to business class to. The sort of person receptionists gave room numbers to.

The sort of person who didn't take no for an answer!

She had found the perfect outfit that would establish from the outset that she meant business. When Finn had seen her in the black Armani he had called her a ball-breaker—she hoped he would get this not-so-subliminal message today!

Seeing Finn wasn't something she wanted to do—in fact she felt sick to her stomach every time she thought about it—but this was the sort of occasion when a good sister put aside her personal feelings. She had to do this for Annie's sake.

Annie had made her swear she wouldn't tell Connor—her sister wasn't thinking very rationally at the moment, but Lucy wasn't going to tell Connor, she was going to tell Finn.

Lucy frowned; first she had to get to see him. She had discovered, courtesy of the business pages of a broadsheet, that he was in London, and a little more research had revealed where he was staying.

Her expression hardened as she anticipated seeing Finn again. She would never forget the way she'd felt when after not hearing from him for twenty-four hours she had rung the beach house and been told by Bridie that he was too busy to speak to her.

She hadn't believed her—why would she? This was the man who had told her only a week earlier that he wanted her to be part of his life! So she had rung back and insisted she speak to Finn.

'Finn…?'

'Hello, Lucy.'

It was such a relief she didn't notice the lack of warmth in his voice. 'I've been trying to speak to you, but Bridie said you were too busy.'

'Oh. Is there something you wanted?'

'I wanted to talk to you. I miss you, Finn.'

There was a long pause at the other end and if she hadn't been able to hear him breathing she might have thought they'd been cut off.

'Liam was upset that you had left.'

'Oh, I know; give him my love…' Maybe he's not alone, he can't speak freely. She could distinctly recall the thought going through her head. It still hadn't hit her at that point;

she'd been too slow to realise what was happening—she was being dumped.

'I don't think that would be a good idea. In fact I've decided it wouldn't be a good idea if you saw Liam again; you seem to have had quite a disruptive influence on him.'

'You mean the dog?' Even thinking about saying it now made her cringe.

'I don't mean the dog, Lucy, I mean you.'

She actually flinched back as though he'd reached out across the miles and struck her, and in a way he had done.

She rallied a little then and demanded angrily, 'You think I'll settle for sleeping with you when it suits you?'

'Actually, Lucy, I don't want that either.'

She had no recollection of what she'd said then or even if she'd said anything. First of all she'd been numb, then she'd been angry with Finn, of course, but most of all with herself for believing him—for believing what she had wanted to.

The person behind Reception was polite but firm. 'I'm sorry, miss, but we don't give out guests' room numbers.'

'But I'm a *very* close friend—he'll want to see me.'

'I'd be glad to give him a message.' The smartly dressed young man remained impervious to her look of appeal.

'I'd prefer to give him the message personally,' Lucy replied with an admirable display of restraint.

Finn would say I should have made a back-up plan, she thought.

When she had lain in bed imagining her sister lying awake in the next room and formulating her plan she had not imagined failure. Despite the promise Annie had wrung out of her not to tell Connor, Lucy had been determined that the Fitzgeralds would pay for what they had done.

She took a seat in the foyer and was trying to work out

another plan of attack when fate intervened in the shape of a good-looking silver-haired figure in a suit.

Lucy didn't really notice him until she heard the magic words.

'Mr Fitzgerald said you were delayed, sir. He asked me to look out for you. The party is in the Orangery. I'll show the way, shall I?'

Shaking with anticipation, Lucy forced herself to stay a discreet distance behind until the distinguished-looking figure had been shown to a table out of her sight. Then she approached the person waiting to guide guests to their seats. He looked up with a smile.

'The Fitzgerald party?'

'Of course, this way…'

Lucy, who, despite her composed air, had been half expecting to be unmasked as an impostor and asked to leave, couldn't believe it was actually working. Her fierce determination wavered as the reality of what she was doing hit her—she was going to see Finn.

No, I can't do this, her mind screamed. An image of her sister's tear-stained face flashed through her mind and her resolution firmed. She was here for Annie.

Seated around the table there were several people including Finn, three men and two women; the latter, she noted with *purely* academic interest that resembled a knife thrust in the guts, were young and good-looking; all were well dressed and prosperous-looking.

She'd read somewhere recently that women who wore expensive designer clothes were merely using them to hide deep insecurities—if this was right these two were hiding theirs well! They looked incredibly confident and assured, the sort of sophisticated women who could handle the kind of no-strings relationships Finn favoured.

No longer able to delay the moment, Lucy took a deep

breath and allowed her glance to move to Finn himself. He looked very at home in this company and every inch the successful businessman he was, dressed in a stylish charcoal-grey suit and white shirt that emphasised his warm skin tones.

The moment she looked at him her carefully rehearsed speeches were forgotten. She swayed as she was struck by a violent surge of feeling. It was a double whammy, overwhelming lust and tenderness, inextricably linked.

What's wrong, Lucy, afraid to say the words—?

I love Finn Fitzgerald.

Her chest felt as though someone had it in a vice and was squeezing hard. She couldn't breathe.

The only thing she could think about was touching him; she could remember his touch and the way it had made her feel and she wanted to feel it again. The crowning moment of her utter humiliation was when she felt the hot throb between her thighs.

The woman he was talking to casually reached across and touched his arm. Looking at the painted nails against the sober fabric, Lucy experienced a wave of jealousy so intense that she felt physically sick. She pressed her hand to her mouth until the nausea had diminished.

The conversation around the table gradually died away as all eyes turned to the slim, striking young woman dressed in black standing motionless beside the table. Finn, his attention focused politely on the woman to his right, was the last to recognise her presence.

Lucy watched him turn his head, heard the harsh sound of his startled inhalation. In the grip of a strange detachment, she watched the shock wash over his dark face, saw the firm, golden-toned flesh pull tight over his marvellous bones as every inch of him tensed. It was there and then it was gone, the shutters came down and he was in control.

'Lucy…?'

He said it the way you acknowledged someone you saw catching the train to work every day. 'Hello, Finn.'

'This isn't a good time…' he said quietly, his eyes flickering towards the people listening.

Lucy's chin went up; if he thought she was going to hang around until *he* considered it a good time he was about to learn differently.

'Too damned bad!' she declared with a smile.

Her low voice was clear and the acoustics in the room were quite exceptional. The potential for drama was beginning to draw the attention of other tables; several diners were murmuring to one another and glancing surreptitiously across.

Finn looked at her set face for a moment then shrugged. Eyes not leaving hers, he leaned across and spoke to the man seated across from him. Lucy was vaguely aware of this person saying something to his fellow diners.

'Shall we go somewhere a little—?'

'More private? Actually, Finn, I'm quite comfortable here.'

Eyes narrowed, Finn linked his fingers behind his neck and leaned back in his seat. He was not a person inclined to waste his energy on lost causes. He had learnt that it was easier in the long run if you accepted that some things in life you couldn't fight against, some things were inevitable.

It was *inevitable* that Lucy was going to make a scene no matter what actions he took, in fact in his opinion it was likely that trying to stop her would probably only make matters worse. Despite this realisation of horrors to come he felt happier than he had done in weeks. When he analysed the reason for this the answer he got was amazingly simple—he felt good because he was looking at Lucy.

'Can I do something for you, Lucy?'

The fact he looked so damned relaxed only increased Lucy's escalating resentment and anger.

'Yes, you can.' At the last second she hesitated…maybe this wasn't the sort of thing you discussed in public? Was she simply using Annie's situation to excuse her own desire for revenge?

Finn rested his chin on the peak of his steepled fingers. 'It's not like you to be at a loss for words.'

The gentle taunt made her expression harden. 'My sister is pregnant. What are you going to do about it, Finn?'

What her words lacked in subtlety they more than made up for in dramatic impact.

At that point things started happening incredibly quickly, so that when she thought about it later Lucy couldn't be sure of the exact sequence of events.

She registered the collective sharp intake of breath, heard the clatter of a chair being knocked over, saw Finn, his face pale, begin to rise in his seat and sensed movement just out of her line of vision.

'She's pregnant?' The iron-hard fingers on her upper arm dug into her flesh and spun her around before the person who had asked the urgent question took hold of both her arms. 'Annie is expecting a baby, you're sure?'

Dazed, Lucy found herself looking up into the impassioned face of a fierce-looking young man.

So this is Connor.

How strange, she found herself thinking, he wasn't at all the way she'd imagined. In her head she'd supposed her sister's lover was a paler version of Finn, but this man was quite different, and not just facially. Slim and compact in build, he was her own height. His lean dark features were sensitive rather than conventionally handsome and his deep-set eyes were so dark they appeared almost black.

Annie had told her once that Con Fitzgerald had the sweetest smile in the world, but she'd have to take Annie's word for it because he wasn't smiling at that moment.

'You're Lucy; I've seen photos…'

Lucy nodded and tried to pull away but found she couldn't.

'Did she…did Annie send you…?' He spoke in a low, urgent, staccato monotone.

Lucy shook her head, and he closed his eyes and groaned.

'Was she going to tell me?'

Lucy looked into his anguished face and felt her anger slipping away…uncomfortably she shook her head. This was too intense.

'She must hate me,' he whispered. His shocked dark gaze suddenly refocused on Lucy's face. 'Take me to her…make her see me…' Lucy winced as the grip on her shoulders tightened.

'Con, let her go.'

Finn delivered the instruction in a quiet but imperative tone that was in stark contrast to his brother's agitated manner. Lucy was dismayed when his brother appeared not to hear. With an impatient frown he shrugged off the restraining hand on his shoulder.

Finn repeated himself only this time there was an edge of anger in his deep voice. 'I said let her go, Con.' He came up to his brother's side; the younger man looked fragile by comparison, but Lucy was in a position to know Con was no weakling.

For a moment Lucy thought Finn was going to physically haul his brother away. All the ingredients were there for this situation to get seriously out of hand and, as she was the person who had lit the fuse, Lucy knew it was her job to cool things down.

She turned her head. 'Leave him, Finn.' Her eyes found his. 'It's all right...' She exhaled with relief when Finn nodded.

'You're hurting her, Con.'

'What?' His brother looked around in confusion at his deathly pale face.

'You're hurting Lucy.'

Frowning, Con looked at his hands curled around her arms as if they belonged to someone else, then a tide of colour washed over his skin. 'God, I'm sorry!' he cried, looking appalled as he released her and stepped back.

Finn spared his brother a glance before he turned to Lucy. 'Are you all right?'

Lucy nodded and hoped her legs wouldn't collapse under her. Psyching herself up to it then the confrontation itself had been incredibly draining both physically and mentally.

Finn looked sceptical but after scanning her face some of the tension left his lean features.

'Give me five minutes to sort things out here.' He glanced briefly towards the table of silent guests. 'Con will take you up to the suite...' He raised his voice slightly. 'Con?'

His brother nodded.

When he had asked her how she felt Lucy had realised that what she *wasn't* feeling was the way she had expected to. Where was the glow of satisfaction confronting the Fitzgeralds with their disgraceful behaviour was meant to give her?

Actually she felt wretched; Connor might not be her choice of partner for Annie, but from his reaction he was clearly not the uncaring bastard of her imagination. And Finn hadn't got anyone pregnant...maybe that was the problem—deep down she half wished he had!

This unexpected and shocking insight drove the last vestiges of colour from her face.

'*Oh, God!*'

'Pardon?'

Lucy looked up, startled by the sound of Connor's voice. She had no idea how long the lift doors had been open or how long he had been politely waiting there for her to enter. Sympathy washed over her as she looked at him.

'Listen, I'm sorry,' she said awkwardly as the lift began its smooth ascent, 'about the way I told you.' She had started that day so sure that she was doing the right thing for the right reason—now she was a lot less sure on both counts.

'*You've* no need to be sorry.'

'Self-flagellation isn't going to help matters...'

The flicker of a shocked smile that passed across his pale, set features gave Lucy a glimpse of the charm Annie said he possessed.

'Annie said you were blunt.' The amusement left his face. 'How is she...?'

'She's sick in the mornings and her hormones are totally out of whack, but she's coping...'

'She shouldn't have to *cope*!' he gritted angrily. 'I should have been there with her. I love her, you know.' He looked at Lucy as though daring her to contradict him. 'I've acted like a total idiot, because I was scared... I've been married twice, and do you know something that's funny...? I've never been in love before. I was scared stiff. Scared of what I was feeling, but most of all scared of messing up yet again.'

Lucy, who didn't know how to respond to these confidences without sounding trite, took the cowardly route and changed the subject. 'Those people you were dining with...?'

Connor groaned. 'Oh, hell, I'd forgotten about them.'

'Were they important?' She sort of knew the answer before it came.

'You could say that,' Con replied with a dry laugh. 'Finn has spent the past few weeks putting together a deal that could mean a major expansion. It would mean securing the jobs of the people who already work for us, and creating hundreds of new ones. Those people,' he explained gloomily, 'represented all the interested parties...'

Lucy's spirits plummeted to subterranean levels; not only had she rubbished his reputation in public but she had also lost him a dream deal. She was definitely going to be Finn's favourite person!

'It gets better. Conrad Latimer was sitting at the next table.'

'The gossip columnist Conrad Latimer...?'

Connor nodded. 'None other.'

'I suppose it's too much to hope he didn't notice anything?'

CHAPTER THIRTEEN

LIKE the rest of the hotel the furnishings and décor in Finn's suite were a tribute to art deco. Con walked over to the window and just stood there looking out. Lucy's eyes were drawn to the few personal items littered around the room. Somehow it seemed to Lucy that even though he wasn't there Finn's personality was imprinted on the impersonal hotel room.

What am I doing here? she asked herself, looking around. Finn had already made it quite clear there was no place for her in his life and she didn't want him.

'Did she consider...?'

Lucy started at the sound of his driven voice. He couldn't finish but she didn't have any problem interpreting his silence.

'No, Connor, she always wanted the baby, she wants it very much.'

She saw his shoulders sag in relief. 'Does she look...can you tell yet...?' This time there was a hunger for details, not dread, in his voice.

'No, she's not showing; it's far too early. Right now she thinks she looks fat,' Lucy told him with a grin.

'I'm sure she looks beautiful,' Con protested.

'Maybe you should tell her that...?' Lucy suggested gently.

'What do you think, Finn...?'

With a startled intake of breath Lucy spun around. 'Damn shoes!' she cried, lurching sideways to right her balance.

He watched, his expression enigmatic, as she pushed her hair out of her eyes. 'Why don't you take them off? I'm sure you'll be more comfortable.'

Lucy's toes curled inside her shoes…he really did have the most incredibly seductive voice, the sort of voice you felt. She fancied she could feel it humming through her veins.

'When I think of you it's always barefoot, walking on a beach.' One by one the fingers of his clenched fist unfurled and his fingers spread in a gesture that made her think of sand slipping through her fingers.

Their eyes touched and the air was snatched from her lungs in one gasp. The air of suppressed passion emanating from his powerful frame was tangible, the air around him seemed to vibrate with it.

Con, too wrapped up in his own personal drama to notice the electric tension in the air, walked up to his brother. 'I'm going to be a father,' he said in a dazed voice that suggested he still hadn't got his head around it.

Finn reluctantly turned his attention to the younger man but his impatience melted into rueful sympathy when he saw the wonderment in his brother's eyes. 'So it would seem.'

The fact his reply left room for doubt was something that brought Lucy's protective instincts on to full alert.

'There's no *seem, appear* or *possibly* about it. Annie's pregnant and he's the father, unless you are calling me a liar…?'

Con looked shocked at the suggestion. 'Of course he isn't saying that.' He appealed to his brother, saying, 'Are you, Finn?' He didn't give his brother the chance to reply but continued in a distracted voice, 'Do you think I should ring first, or just turn up…?'

'I think you should do what you feel is right.'

'But what do *you* think?'

'I think this is between you and Annie.'

Con appeared to consider this. Then, taking a deep breath, he straightened his shoulders and looked his brother in the eye. 'You're right, I'll just—'

'Good idea.' Finn smiled, steering his brother gently in the direction of the door.

'I never thought he'd go,' Finn breathed, falling full length on the king-sized bed as the door shut behind his brother. He closed his eyes.

A look of total shock spread across Lucy's face as she looked at him lying spread-eagled on the bed. 'I thought you'd want to go with him.'

Finn loosened his tie and opened his eyes. 'To hold his hand…? Believe me, that is what my every instinct is telling me to do,' he revealed surprisingly.

'But you didn't?'

'Someone told me I should back off and let the man fix his own stuff when it breaks. Besides, I didn't think it would impress your sister if I tagged along and I guess I've got to stop trying to make up for the fact Mom chose me not him some time. Yeah,' he said in response to her startled look, 'I worked it out without the assistance of a therapist too…impressive, don't you think…?'

Lucy chose to respond to the least provocative of his comments. 'Since when did you listen to advice?' Then in a louder voice, 'You really shouldn't be wearing your shoes—you'll ruin that quilt.'

'You bother about the oddest things,' he observed, looking amused by her comment—a comment that Lucy still couldn't believe she'd voiced. 'You take them off for me if you're so worried.'

The offer brought Lucy's alarmed eyes to his face.

'Unless you consider that task too demeaning.'

Demeaning she could deal with, but getting excited about taking someone's shoes off, even if they were hand-stitched Italian leather, put *her* in the category of needing therapy. Maybe this was how fetishes started…?

'I might not be able to stop there once I start.' It had seemed a great idea in theory to turn her real fears into a joke, but she hadn't allowed for a voice that was little more than a shocked, breathy whisper.

'I usually start at the top and work my way down but I'm very adaptable.'

She didn't even look at him.

'Don't even go there, Finn,' she muttered grimly. 'Not after what you did.'

His reply was almost too soft for her to hear. 'You're just delaying the inevitable, you know, sweetheart.'

And she was going to carry on doing so for as long as possible.

'There'll be plenty of opportunity for cosy little chats like this in the future, seeing as there's a strong possibility that we're going to be related whether we like it or not,' Finn observed, lifting a lazy arm above his head. 'Always supposing Annie will have him. What's your reading on that…?'

Lucy's soft mouth formed a rueful smile as she willed some of the tension to leave her body. 'Oh, she'll have him.' Her brows drew together in a line of anxiety. 'Should you have let him go like that…?' she persisted worriedly. 'I mean, he looked so…' She looked at his recumbent form with a critical frown. 'I can't believe you're taking this so calmly.'

Finn's eyes opened, and she saw that the restive glitter in their depths was in stark contrast to his indolent pose.

'The guy has just learnt he's about to become a father—how do you expect him to look?' The ironic enquiry

brought a flush to her cheeks. 'Besides, Con is tougher than
he looks. Which is just as well, considering the way you
dropped that little bombshell.'

Embarrassed, Lucy moved away, aware of his blue eyes
trained on her as she walked across the room. 'If I'd known
he was there I wouldn't have—'

'Staged that little scene? It was very impressive, by the
way. Looking out for family is a good thing, but one thing
puzzled me.'

'Only one…you're lucky,' she responded drily. 'Just
about everything puzzles me.'

'That's because you're in denial. Things fall into place
when you quit fighting it.'

What had Finn been fighting? 'I'm not in denial.'

'Why was *I* the target of your wrath?'

'You weren't.'

'But you just said you didn't know Con was there…'

'Annie made me promise not to tell him.'

'So you thought you'd let me do that and the public
humiliation was a bonus.'

'Yes, it was, and you deserved to be humiliated after the
way you treated me…' She stopped as her voice developed
a weak, tearful quality.

She didn't just want Finn to know he'd hurt her, she
wanted him to see she'd come out the other side and she
didn't need him any more. This, of course, would have been
easier if she hadn't just realised that she loved him.

'Connor told me who those people were.' She wanted
revenge but not at any cost.

To her astonishment Finn dismissed this critical deal
with a shrug of his impressive shoulders. 'That situation is
retrievable. So let's talk about this situation.'

'Like you said, that's up to Annie and Con now.'

'Con and Annie. I'm as much into family feeling as you

are,' he gritted, pushing his fingers deep into his dark hair and dragging it back from his forehead. 'Aren't I allowed some time to think about what I'd like in my life?' he demanded.

'A life in which I have no place, as you made crystal-clear.' And don't you ever forget it, Lucy.

'I was late for that meeting you gate-crashed.'

Lucy stared ahead, stony-faced, not looking as he levered himself into a sitting position.

'You haven't asked me why.'

'I'm not going to.'

'You not going to look at me either?'

'No.' Why put herself through that sort of pain?

'I got this phone call from Bridie earlier today.'

'How nice for you.'

'She couldn't live with her guilt; she needed to confess.'

'You wouldn't be my first choice as stand-in priest.'

'Did you leave Ireland because your sister needed you, Lucy?'

'You know I did,' she cried, forgetting her decision not to look at him.

'Actually I didn't, not until today. When I arrived at the beach house and you weren't there Bridie explained that you got bored and decided to leave early, but you *might* ring some time.'

The colour fled from Lucy's face as she sank down weakly onto the edge of the bed. 'I asked her...' She pressed a hand to her mouth to hold in the sob she felt forming in her aching throat.

'To tell me that your sister was ill. I guess,' he said half to himself, 'that translates as pregnant.'

'I didn't know then,' she told him in a bemused voice. 'Annie didn't tell me until I got back...'

'To make matters worse,' he continued, 'Liam seemed

to have fallen in love with you—I guess it's a case of like father like son—but the fact you'd made my kid love you and then skipped out, or so I thought, without an explanation just because you were bored made me pretty damned mad.'

Lucy stared at him, her mouth hanging open as he pulled the smart silk tie from around his neck and threw it across the room. 'You're not in love with me,' she felt impelled to point out.

'That's one thing you should know about me from the outset, sweetheart: I react very badly to being contradicted. I always think I'm right, though actually in this case I am. If I didn't love you, my dear, sweet, adorable Lucy why would I have gone home carrying a great damned rock in my pocket?'

Before her disbelieving eyes he withdrew a velvet box from his trouser pocket and flung it down on the bed in front of her.

'It won't bite—take a look,' he suggested softly. Still she didn't move. 'I thought I was doing fine, I thought my life was all right—better than all right actually—but it wasn't. It took meeting you to make me see that. My life needs fixing, Lucy. You got any ideas…?'

She did, she had lots, but none she dared believe. Lucy picked up the box and slowly opened it. The square-cut emerald that stared back at her made her gasp. 'Oh, Finn, it's beautiful,' she cried.

Finn took the ring from the box and slid it on her finger. It fitted perfectly. 'About these repairs to my life…?'

The tenderness on his face brought tears to her eyes. 'What did you have in mind?'

'This.'

He kissed her with a ravenous hunger that she responded to with wholehearted enthusiasm. When they broke apart he brushed the hair from her face and held it between his big hands.

'I love you... Oh, God, Finn...!' she gasped suddenly.

'What's wrong, sweetheart?'

'There's something you don't know...'

'It doesn't matter,' he said, pressing a series of open-mouthed kisses to the smooth column of her neck.

'Stop that,' she begged. 'This is important.'

He stopped doing what he was. 'Do you love me?'

'God, yes!'

'Then it's not important,' he said, carrying on where he'd left off.

'I appreciate your priorities, I really do, but...' If she didn't tell him now she could see it would be a long time before she did. He had to know; there might be some way he could limit the damage. 'That gossip columnist...'

'Conrad Latimer?'

'You knew he was there.'

With a sigh Finn reluctantly stopped what he was doing. 'I did.'

'Will it be *very* harmful to your business interests if he writes things about you?'

'Of course, in an ideal world you avoid getting your name plastered across gossip columns, but when that isn't possible...'

'Like now?'

'Like now,' he agreed, 'the trick is getting them to write what you want them to without them realising what you're doing.'

Lucy listened to his matter-of-fact explanation with a fascinated expression. 'Is that what you've done?'

'You'd better ring your sister before tomorrow...it might be best if she doesn't read about our wedding in the tabloids.'

'You told him we were getting married!' she gasped. 'How could you…? You hadn't even…we…what would you have done if I'd said no?'

'It wasn't an option. Oh, by the way, when he asked me what you did I explained you were an incredibly talented new author and that several publishers were even now involved in a bidding war for your first novel.'

'Finn, you *didn't*…! But they're not.'

'No, but as soon as they read that they will be; that's the way the world works, Lucy, my love.'

'But it might be awful.'

'Writer's insecurity,' he said knowledgeably. 'Why don't you let the readers decide?'

'I haven't even finished it yet!' she exclaimed.

'No, but you'll have to now, won't you?'

Lucy stared at him. 'That's why you did it, didn't you…you manipulative snake…?'

'I'm *your* manipulative snake.'

Suddenly the sheer joy of loving him and being loved by him blazed through her and her indignation fell away. 'I love you, Finn.'

'And I love you,' he rasped, hauling her roughly into his arms. 'When I think of these last few weeks,' he groaned.

'Don't think about them,' Lucy commanded, placing a finger to his lips. 'Think about the future—you, me and Liam.' She was relieved to see the dark shadows retreat from his eyes.

'And dog.'

'Oh, yes, dog. He hasn't got a name yet, then?'

'No, *he* hasn't, but the puppies have, all five of them.'

'Puppies? But he's—'

'A she,' Finn cut in, grinning at her startled expression. 'If you didn't notice that, my love, you are in serious need of some tuition in the anatomy department.'

'Know anyone qualified to tutor me?' she asked, lying back in what she hoped was a provocative pose.

'Now that you mention it...when would you like these sessions to start?'

'I thought they already had,' Lucy gasped as his hand closed over her breast.

'I'm glad you noticed that.' His eyes darkened as she writhed with pleasure. 'One of the more obvious differences... Did I mention that Liam christened the runt of the litter Lucy?'

Lucy grabbed his head and yanked him down to her. 'Kiss me before I get bored.'

With a throaty laugh Finn obliged, and as Lucy gave herself up to the magic of being loved the way only Finn could, she realised that she was never going to be bored again.

eHARLEQUIN.com

The Ultimate Destination for Women's Fiction

Visit eHarlequin.com's Bookstore today for today's most popular books at great prices.

- An extensive selection of romance books by top authors!
- Choose our convenient "bill me" option. No credit card required.
- New releases, Themed Collections and hard-to-find backlist.
- A sneak peek at upcoming books.
- Check out book excerpts, book summaries and Reader Recommendations from other members and post your own too.
- Find out what everybody's reading in Bestsellers.
- Save BIG with everyday discounts and exclusive online offers!
- Our Category Legend will help you select reading that's exactly right for you!
- Visit our Bargain Outlet often for huge savings and special offers!
- Sweepstakes offers. Enter for your chance to win special prizes, autographed books and more.

Your purchases are 100% guaranteed—so shop online at www.eHarlequin.com today!

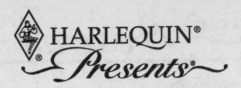

HARLEQUIN®
Presents®

The world's bestselling romance series...
The series that brings you your favorite authors,
month after month:

Helen Bianchin...Emma Darcy
Lynne Graham...Penny Jordan
Miranda Lee...Sandra Marton
Anne Mather...Carole Mortimer
Susan Napier...Michelle Reid

and many more uniquely talented authors!

Wealthy, powerful, gorgeous men...
Women who have feelings just like your own...
The stories you love, set in exotic, glamorous locations...

HARLEQUIN®
Presents®

Seduction and Passion Guaranteed!